FURIOUS
OLD WOMEN

FURIOUS
OLD WOMEN

LEO BRUCE

ACADEMY
CHICAGO

Copyright © 1960 by Propertius Company, Ltd.

This edition published in 1983 by Academy Chicago Publishers
An imprint of Chicago Review Press Incorporated
814 North Franklin Street
Chicago, Illinois 60610
ISBN 978-0-89733-084-8

Library of Congress Cataloging-in-Publication Data
Bruce, Leo. 1903-1980.
        Furious old women.

        I. Title.
PR6005.R673 F8 1983 b 823'.912 83-15683
ISBN 0-89733-084-6 (pbk.)

Cover design: Sadie Teper
Cover photography: Krisztina Papp

Printed in the United States of America

1

"ANGRY young men?" said Mrs Bobbin. "Ridiculous. Whining about their maladjustment or disillusionment or whatnot. I'm seventy-one years old, I lost my husband in the first world war, my only son in the second, and my income has been whittled down to a pittance. Now my sister has been battered to death by hooligans. If I were to start talking the self-pitying rubbish of these people there might be some reason for it. But I don't and if I hear or read another word about 'the beat generation' I shall scream. Quite literally, wherever I happen to be. Now give me a cigarette and tell me how you're going to find out who murdered Millicent."

Carolus Deene looked at the old lady appreciatively. Seventy-one, was she? She looked twelve years younger and when she snorted as she did now she made one think of a war-horse.

"Well, I'm going to start by asking you some questions."

"That won't get you far. I was in London at the time as I've told you. But ask what you like. If it's only to satisfy my curiosity I must know who killed Milly."

"She was the eldest of you?"

"Yes. I came second, my brother Arthur third—he died in 1940—and Flora was the youngest. She was a late child and is only fifty-four."

"You three sisters lived together?"

"We had done since the war, when I gave up my London flat and came down here."

"This village was your family home?"

"Yes. We were all born here. Nothing feudal but we have lived in this house, Crossways, for three generations.

5

Millicent and Flora never really left it. They were always wrapped up in parish affairs. I married in 1910 and didn't return till my son was killed in 1940. I couldn't afford to keep a home of my own and joined my sisters."

"You liked living here?"

"Bored stiff," said Mrs Bobbin. "Church affairs meant nothing to me and my sisters were immersed in them. Local residents pretentious and unintelligent. I was almost reduced to television. As I say, I have a right to be annoyed with life."

"But you had no financial worries?"

"Hadn't we? You didn't know Millicent. She had most of the money, the largest share from my father and a big sum from my brother's estate. Flora and I had meagre little incomes, yet Millicent insisted that we should all pay the same share. She had played the stock market for twenty years and had made herself an extremely rich woman. But you'd never have known it. Every single household expense was divided into three equal parts and we all shelled out the same. I haven't had a penny to play with, *really* play with, since the very fair income left me by my husband has dwindled to nothing. I may not have been in want or hunger perhaps but there are worse things than those. There is perpetual niggling, calculating and balancing which goes on for years and never leaves one any room for a small extravagance. We had that here at Crossways."

"Will your sister's death relieve you of it?"

"I don't know. The will is enormous and very complicated and most of her wealth seems to be going to help Milly's pet church charities. But this money is so tied up with conditions on how the church is to be run that it will produce problems of its own. There's some for Flora and me but I don't know yet how much. Certainly not enough to compensate us for the annoyance of the murder."

"Annoyance, Mrs Bobbin?"

"I'm extremely angry about it. Milly may have been mean and sanctimonious but she was my sister. To club her to death on her way to church was quite damnable."

"You said 'on her way to church'. What makes you think that?"

"Her body was found in an open grave in the churchyard. Dug for a Mr Chilling, I believe, a retired shopkeeper who lived in the village."

"Yes, but it might have been taken there, surely?"

"I don't think so. You will find as you come to look into this that the whole thing's bound up with the church, just as my sister was."

"Even so, what makes you say 'on her way' to church? She may have been coming away from it."

Mrs Bobbin thought for a minute, then said, indifferently, "I suppose so."

"It happened about a week ago?"

"Today's Friday, so it was eight days ago. Last Thursday, February 18th. It was a dry cold day which grew cloudy in the afternoon so that the night was dark. I went up to London by the ten o'clock train in the morning and got back at eight-fifteen. I walked from the station and let myself in to find the house completely dark and empty. I at once telephoned the police."

"No one normally slept in the house but the three of you?"

"No one. Our only domestic help is a young woman called Naomi who comes in during the day and leaves after lunch. I suppose we are lucky to have her."

"Local girl?"

"Yes. Naomi Chester. I often wondered why she stayed with us. Millicent was unbearable with her."

"In what way?"

"Inquisitive. My sister, Mr Deene, had rather a nasty mind and a habit of prying into other people's lives. Naomi's was a sad case. She is in love with a young man called Grey who married about three years ago a girl who has since been certified insane. There is a small child

7

by the marriage and it appears that Naomi is going to have a baby by Grey. My sister's curiosity about this embarrassed us all, particularly Naomi. But I suppose the girl continued to work for us to remain in the village near Grey. My sister Flora and I were quite fond of her."

"Where was your sister Flora on the day of the murder?"

"She left the house during the afternoon and went by bus to Burley, the nearest town. She did some shopping, had tea at a café then went to the pictures. She got in soon after I did."

"When did you first hear of your sister's death?"

"Not till next day. We had a most worrying night, of course. It appears that next morning the sexton, a man called Rumble, who works for us in his spare time as a gardener, noticed that the grave he had dug for Chilling had been partly filled in and began to investigate. He found my sister's body loosely covered with earth."

Carolus Deene nodded.

"That was ingenious," he said. "If it hadn't been noticed and the coffin lowered the chances are the body would never have been found. It would have been just another mysterious disappearance."

"But not quite ingenious enough. Why didn't the murderers dig deeper? Then they *would* have got away with it."

"Who was the last person to see your sister alive?"

"So far as we know, Naomi Chester. She usually leaves the house about two-thirty but was later that day. She says that there was nothing unusual when she went. My sister Flora had already caught the 2.40 bus for Burley so that when Naomi went Millicent was left alone in the house. But that was not unusual. Any one of the three of us was quite accustomed to being alone. It's always been a very quiet and orderly village."

"So nothing is known of your sister's movements after Naomi Chester left her here?"

"Unless the police have discovered anything. But it's

8

fairly easy to guess. My sister decided to go round to the church."

"There was no service?"

"I think not. Mr Waddell, the vicar, did once try to introduce what he called daily evensong but the attendance was so small he had to give it up. No, I think Millicent went there for one of her chores—cleaning the brass or something."

"Flowers, perhaps?"

"No. She disapproved of flowers in church. Millicent was what is called Low Church. Flowers were only a shade worse than candles which were anathema, while as for incense . . . However, you'll hear all that in good time. She must have gone to polish her brass—she took a pride in an idiotic-looking eagle that served as a lectern—and on her way was clubbed and robbed. As simple as that."

"But was she known to carry anything worth robbing?"

"She had a rather ostentatious taste in jewellery. There were usually enough diamonds on her to make a fair-sized tiara. And she nearly always carried a fairly large sum of money."

"Both had been stolen, I take it, when the corpse was found?"

"Oh yes. I've told you she was done to death by hooligans. Damnable."

"How did she carry the money?"

"It was my sister's habit to carry a most capacious bag. More like a shopping basket, I often told her. In this was her purse. The bag was found with her body but the purse was missing."

"Nothing has been recovered?"

"Certainly not. The police say they are investigating but beyond asking me a number of questions even more moronic than yours they have done nothing to my knowledge. That is why when Mrs Kensington said she knew you I told her to ring you up. I want someone hanged for this. Yes, Mr Deene, hanged by the neck till

9

he's thoroughly well dead. I have never been more infuriated in my life. Have a drink? "

"Thank you."

"Whisky? "

"Yes, please."

"I'll get it for you. Flora's still more or less prostrate with shock and Naomi left hours ago."

"Naomi Chester is still working for you, then? "

"Why not? She inherited nothing from Millicent and she's got her coming child to think of."

Sipping his whisky and looking about him Carolus saw no sign of the 'meagre little incomes' 'whittled down to a pittance' and 'dwindling to nothing'. They sat in the central room of the house from which a fine stone staircase curved upward to the first floor far above them. The furniture was of the eighteenth century, sherry-dark mahogany beautifully polished, and there were several good portraits.

"It is only since my sister's death that I am able to offer you a drink in this house. Millicent was quite rabid on the subject. Not a drop of alcohol must cross the door. I often wondered whether she had some secret temptation to drink. Such violent opinions often mean that, I'm told. I drink very little myself so it was no sacrifice to me, and Millicent carried Flora with her in this as in most other things. But I like to be able to offer ordinary hospitality."

Carolus said he appreciated it.

"Does the case interest you? " asked Mrs Bobbin sharply.

"Yes. But there are one or two things I should tell you before we go any farther. First, I do not necessarily accept your view that your sister was clubbed to death by ruffians for the sake of immediate robbery."

"Why not? "

"It doesn't quite ring true. That kind of murder could happen here I suppose, as it could happen anywhere in the world, but all my instincts are against it. And I don't think thugs of that kind would have waited to cover the body at the bottom of an open grave. It's not impossible but I don't *think* that's the way it happened."

"Go on," commanded Mrs Bobbin.

Carolus looked at her strong resolute face and beautiful white hair and tried not to make his words sound opinionated and peremptory.

"You see, I think it could have happened almost anywhere. It was, as you say, a dark night and there would have been plenty of time to take your sister's body to the churchyard and cover it, for persons who knew that the grave was already dug. Moreover the actual killing could have been the work of anyone—even a woman."

"You seem to wish to widen the possibilities instead of narrowing them."

"Well, they are pretty wide. I take it there isn't much known even about the time of your sister's death?"

"I believe not. She had been under the earth for some hours."

"So we do not know when, why, where or by whom."

"If you put it like that. . . ."

"Then another thing I must tell you. I can't give much time at present to investigation. The Spring term is a month old and as you know I'm a schoolmaster. I think the police will get at the truth long before I shall."

"They may. But I'm prepared to chance that. I have one thing in common with your angry young men, Mr Deene—I do not like policemen. They are paid to protect the public and their failure to do so in the last twenty years has turned the country into a paradise for criminals while decent citizens who overstep some silly little law are harassed and persecuted. I believe the police are often corrupt and unscrupulous and I'm almost as angry when I think of their failure in this affair as when I think of the murderer's success. If the police should hit on a solution before you it will either be a miracle or a mistake. So go ahead even if it's a part-time job with you."

"Your sister will wish that, too?"

11

"My sister is just as angry as I am over this. Perhaps angrier, in an Old Testament sort of way. She's calling for vengeance like someone on Mount Sinai. She will be delighted if you help to discover the murderer. So far as we're concerned you have a free hand. The case is wide open."

"It certainly is. I have never approached anything with such a range of possibilities. If one doesn't accept the theory of robbery one can't even see a motive."

"I wouldn't say that. A number of people will benefit financially by my sister's death. I myself, my sister Flora, our nephew Dundas Griggs, the vicar Bonar Waddell and a former chauffeur of my father's who keeps one of the local inns, a man named George Larkin. He has a son called Bill who is also, rather unaccountably, in the will."

"Quite a collection."

"But as I've told you I'm convinced that there was nothing like a motive beyond the immediate one of robbery."

"Had your sister any enemies?"

Mrs Bobbin considered this for a moment.

"I'm tempted to say 'No' because the enemies she had are so obviously unconnected with the case. But there are two women in the village who hated Millicent and believe me, Mr Deene, in a little community like this hate can be fierce. One was the vicar's wife, Agatha Waddell. I suppose it was some kind of jealousy because her husband gave a good deal of time and attention to Millicent. Agatha is a lean and hungry-looking woman who seems thoroughly dissatisfied with life."

"And the second?"

"The second is Grazia Vaillant, the vicar's *other* best parishioner. I told you my sister's life turned on the parish."

"Tell me a little about this lady."

"Grazia Vaillant, like Millicent, is rich and immersed in church affairs. Each of these women wanted her own way. But there the similarity ends. Where Millicent was downright Grazia is gushing. Millicent was Low Church, Grazia, High, which left the vicar torn between them trying to look both ways at once. Grazia is somewhat eccentric, Millicent was outwardly rather a common-place woman. Needless to say they detested one another."

" Have you seen Miss Vaillant since your sister's death? "

" Yes. Rather subdued, oddly enough. I think she misses Millicent's opposition. Flora will be no match for her, so she'll get it all her own way and the church will become so High it will stink of incense."

" You speak as though your vicar had nothing to say in the matter? "

" What could he do between two women like Millicent and Grazia? His great ambition is to be all things to all men, a good mixer, popular, tolerant—you know the type. Grazia will bowl him over like a ninepin. As for the curate, he's considered ' good with boys '. Scouts and that."

" Who else is on the parochial scene? "

" Only one Churchwarden who counts—Commander Fyfe. He's not what you would imagine a retired Naval Officer to be like. Then there's Rumble who is both verger and sexton and who found the body. You'll meet him for yourself. I won't spoil your first impressions."

" Who else am I likely to meet? "

" The publican of the Black Horse, George Larkin. Perhaps you had better hear straight away what someone in the village is bound to tell you sooner or later, that is that when he was chauffeur to my father many years ago there was a scandal of some sort. I was at boarding school at the time and have never from that day to this heard the story in full but I believe he ran away with Millicent. My father found them a week later down at Brighton and everything was hushed up. Larkin had a pub bought for him up in Westmorland or somewhere on condition that he did not return here. He waited till after my father's death then returned, since this is after all his native place. His own pub had flourished and he bought the Black

13

Horse. He is a widower now and in his seventies though his son is barely twenty."

"Anyone else?"

"Oh, the village has the usual local characters. Rather irritating, most of them, I find. There's a poacher called Mugger who is rather notorious. The village policeman, Slatt, I consider to be of sub-normal intelligence but doubtless I'm prejudiced. You'll come on others unless you produce a solution almost at once."

"I don't think that's likely. It's all too vague."

"But tempting?"

"Yes."

"Then do your damnedest. Because, as I say, I'm furious. This is the *end*. I've been pretty annoyed for years with this silliness called modern life. It irritates me to make no progress at all except towards old age. I could strangle the self-pitying young people who moan at the mess around them and do nothing about it. But I've never yet been angry on a personal score, I mean at something which happened to me. When I hear that my elder sister has been battered to death and thrown in an open grave, I find it too much. I'm livid. So don't take too long in solving the thing. I understand you're clever. For goodness' sake show it. And help yourself to another drink—don't sit looking at an empty glass."

"Thank you."

"When will you start your enquiries?"

"Tomorrow," said Carolus.

2

CAROLUS drove the forty miles from the village of Gladhurst to the town of Newminster where, in the Queen's School, he was Senior History Master.

The Queen's School, Newminster, is, as its pupils find themselves under the necessity rather often of explaining, a public school. A minor, a small, a lesser-known one, they concede, but still in the required category. It has a hundred and sixty day-boys, ninety boarders and a staff of eighteen. Its buildings are old, picturesque and very unhygienic and one of its class-rooms is a show-piece untouched from the Elizabethan Age in which the school was founded.

At the school Carolus occupied an equivocal position. He was an extraordinarily good teacher but as a member of the staff he gave the headmaster, Mr Gorringer, many unquiet hours. His excessively large private income and Bentley Continental motor-car, his habit of dressing rather too well and keeping up an extravagant establishment for himself did not endear him to the staff, who were sparsely paid, conscientious men. His known interest in criminology and the fact that he had solved a number of much-publicized murder mysteries made the headmaster 'tremble', as he put it, for the good name of the school.

Carolus, moreover, had an unfortunately casual manner which Mr Gorringer could not but feel only narrowly missed the disrespectful. Mr Gorringer took his headmastership seriously and was highly averse to the flippancy of Carolus. He was a large man with a pale solemn face and a magnificent pair of pendulous, hairy ears. His verbose and earnest manner of speech became him.

Carolus was aware that in school the boys were apt to take advantage of his known interest in crime both ancient and modern. A master with a hobby-horse is easily led away from the tiresome lesson in hand into the realms of his fancy. He may or may not realize this as the end of the school period comes and he finds that he has talked for three-quarters of an hour on his favourite subject and forgotten what he was supposed to be teaching.

Carolus Deene was very well aware of his weakness but he regarded his twin interests of crime and history as almost indistinguishable. The history of men is the

15

history of their crimes, he said. Crippen and Richard III, Nero and the latest murderer to be given headlines in newspapers were all one to him, as his pupils delightedly discovered. However Carolus enjoyed his job of teaching history and was conscientious over his work.

As he reached Newminster he realized that it was nearly nine o'clock and expected no mercy from his housekeeper Mrs Stick. The dinner she had cooked for him would be spoilt and her temper with it. If in addition she suspected that his lateness was caused by anything connected with criminal investigation she would be nearly as angry as Mrs Bobbin.

"Fortunately it was chops," she said breathing hard when Carolus was seated. She was a small, thin severe woman who cooked superbly and with her husband made Carolus's home the most comfortable in Newminster.

"That's all right then," said Carolus brightly.

"It's a good thing I didn't put them on," said Mrs Stick. "Nor the soufflay either. Else they'd have been ruined. It's nine o'clock."

"Is it really? Time goes by when you're interested, doesn't it?"

This earned him a long suspicious stare from Mrs Stick.

"I don't know what you've got to be interested in, I'm sure," she said. "It wasn't anything to do with the school because Stick heard tonight from the school porter that you were Missed at the house match this afternoon. The headmaster was enquiring for you afterwards."

"Oh dear, was there a house match?"

"Yes, Sir, there was, and you wasn't at it so when you say you've been interested you can't blame me if I think the worst."

Carolus said nothing while Mrs Stick was bringing in his grilled chops.

"All my nice saltay potatoes have gone dead and greasy, of course. Well, you can't expect anything else. I was only saying to Stick that I don't mind as long as it doesn't

16

mean you're thinking of starting anything of *that* kind again. We can't have murderers and such all over the house."

"Surely we never have?"

"Well, coming here at all hours and us not knowing whether you'd ever come back alive each time you go out. Look at that time they tried to poison you! And how our holiday was upset that year when they kept finding bodies."

"The chops are excellent, Mrs Stick."

"So they may be. But I was saying to Stick today I shan't be cooking for Mr Deene much longer if he gets up to any more of these larks with murderers. It will never do, I said. People will begin to think there's something funny about *us* next."

"And what did Stick say?" asked Carolus curiously, for in all the years he had been hearing of Mrs Stick's remarks to her husband he had never once been supplied with the reply.

"Stick says what *I* say," said Mrs Stick vehemently, and Carolus did not doubt it.

"I don't think there's much fear of your being involved this time, Mrs Stick."

"Then you *are* up to something," said the little woman triumphantly. "I knew it as soon as you came in late like that. Not that poor lady battered to death over at Gladhurst, is it?"

"You wouldn't want to see an elderly woman murdered and the murderer go unpunished, would you?"

"There's police to see to that and no call for you to start upsetting us all. It's no good, Sir. Stick and I will have to leave and go somewhere where we don't have the horrors every day of our lives. Put into an open grave, wasn't she? Look at that and tell me how I'm expected to sleep sound at night. Besides, there's what my sister will say. Last time I saw her she was on about my working where there are all these murders. I don't know. I really don't."

But Carolus had an even more difficult interview next morning when Mr Gorringer the headmaster sent for him during the Break.

Carolus was speeding towards the common-room in order to seize *The Times* before Hollingbourne could despoil the virginity of its crossword puzzle with the two clues he usually managed to solve, when he was waylaid by Muggeridge, the school porter.

"He wants you," said Muggeridge sulkily, not needing to enlarge on this.

"Damn," said Carolus.

"I know. That's what I said when he rang that blasted bell of his." Muggeridge found his life a wearisome one and resented the uniform, including a gold-braided top-hat, on which Mr Gorringer insisted. "He could just as well have come and spoken to you himself. But no, he has to sit at his blasted desk and ring his blasted bell and send me chasing all over the blasted place looking for you while my tea's getting cold. He's got something up his sleeve, too."

"Thank you, Muggeridge."

"Oh, I don't blame *you*," conceded Muggeridge. "You can't help it any more than what I can if he wants to get on his high horse. I shall tell him, one of these days."

Carolus found Mr Gorringer if not on his high horse at least very upright and pontifical as he sat at his enormous study table.

"Ah, Deene," he greeted Carolus in a manner neither over-friendly nor hostile. It was hard to guess what direction the interview would take. "I wanted a word with you."

Carolus nodded.

"Pray take a seat," said Mr Gorringer. "We were disappointed not to see you at the house match yesterday. A very creditable show on the part of Plantagenet." The houses at the Queen's School, Newminster, apart from

18

School House, were known as Plantagenet and Stuart. "But doubtless you had more pressing matters to attend to?"

"Yes," said Carolus.

"It is in some way connected with this that I wished to see you. I cannot help feeling, my dear Deene, that, while you carry out your duties as Senior History Master with conspicuous care and success, your interest in what we might call the life of the school is apt to wander into regions remote from ours. I recognize your right to occupy your own time as you wish but it has come to my ears that the other men are a trifle hurt by your indifference to our extra-academic activities."

Carolus waited.

"It happens, though, that a situation has arisen which will solve this little difficulty in a way most satisfactory to us all. *Breadman has decided to retire.*"

For a moment Carolus did not catch the awful implications of these last five words.

"As you know, he has been at the school as boy and master since the turn of the century and his going will leave a gap difficult indeed to fill. It will also mean that Plantagenet House will require a housemaster. You, Deene, are Breadman's successor by right of seniority and I have decided to appoint you."

Carolus gasped.

"You will have the care of twenty-five boys together with their boarding fees which after due allowance for generous catering leave a very satisfactory balance to your benefit. You will thus, I hope, be drawn into the integral life of the school. Allow me to be the first to congratulate you on this promotion."

"But headmaster, you can't possibly be serious," said Carolus. "As a widower . . ."

"I have considered that. While it is admittedly desirable that our housemasters should be married men, I have decided not to allow this to bar your way. A good housekeeper can surely be found."

19

" But it's quite outside my scope. I know nothing about catering. I couldn't think of accepting the responsibility."

" Come, come, Deene. You are too modest. You will find that once ensconced in Plantagenet you will be absorbed by the small problems it will produce."

" No! " said Carolus desperately. " Let me make it clear at once, headmaster. I appreciate your confidence in me but I decline absolutely."

Mr Gorringer eyed him with severity.

" Surely I am not to understand, Deene, that your personal, perhaps I may be permitted to say selfish, interests stand in the way? Your unfortunate hobby, for instance? If I thought *that* . . ."

Carolus had a sudden inspiration.

" What about Hollingbourne? " he asked. " He's a family man. Catering for twenty-five more beyond his own children would be child's play to him. He'd *like* it."

" Hollingbourne is your junior on the staff," said Mr Gorringer dubiously.

Carolus followed up his advantage.

" Does that really matter? It's right up his street. I couldn't possibly deprive him of it."

" I should like to say that is generous of you, Deene. But I fear me that it is far otherwise. However, Hollingbourne certainly would be gratified by the opportunity. I shall have to consider it."

Carolus found perspiration on his forehead when he left the headmaster's study.

But it was a half holiday and though a bitterly cold day the air was crisp and clean. Carolus decided to drive over to Gladhurst immediately after lunch.

He found the case as put to him by the irate old lady Mrs Bobbin was an unusually intriguing one. There had been a marked inconsistency in her account of it to Carolus yesterday, which he had noted at the time and now reconsidered. While insisting more than once that her sister had met her death at the hands of hooligans

20

whose motive was robbery, she had said twice that he would find it a 'parish' affair and had spoken of the various persons connected with the parish whom he would meet. It was difficult to know what the old lady really believed.

He had read the newspaper account of the inquest and found that this, like everything else connected with the thing, was inconclusive. The injuries to the skull from which Millicent Griggs had died could have been caused by her being struck from behind with something like a club or could be the result of her head striking something immovable with sufficient force. There was almost no indication of the time of death but the body had been covered for at least ten hours when it was found by Rumble in the morning. No weapon had been found and nothing to indicate where Millicent Griggs had met her death. Nobody strange to the village had been observed that afternoon. Nothing had been traced of the jewellery Millicent Griggs had worn nor the money she was carrying.

So the horizon was clear. Not only was there no hint of the murderer's identity—it could not even be guessed whether there had been one or two or even more concerned in the crime. The time of it was unknown, so was the place. The way in which the woman was killed, the weapon, all the information which an investigator usually had at the outset was totally lacking. The only thing on which there seemed to be agreement was motive, but here Carolus found himself highly sceptical of the general conclusion, that Millicent Griggs had been murdered for the jewels and money she carried. It could be but it seemed a trite and unlikely solution.

Yet this did not mean that the case would prove to be extraordinarily baffling. It might even be better to start in such uncertainty. Facts would come with time.

He stopped at a point about a mile from Gladhurst from which the little village could be seen nestling— there was no other word—in its wooded valley. The clear winter afternoon gave its outlines sharpness, the square-towered church, the red roofs, the smoke curling upward. It looked compact as though its houses were huddling together to keep warm. It looked friendly, too, a Christmas card village in which one would have supposed there lived only jovial farmers and their amiable workers, kindly cosy people with no enmity or cruelty among them. Well, he had known scenes like that before and seen the outwardly cheery people he met turn into malicious, jealous and violent brutes before his eyes.

For one moment he hesitated. He had a strange superstitious feeling that ahead of him lay great evil and perhaps danger, that the death of Millicent Griggs, horrible though it was, would prove to be only a part of something more menacing and beastly, and that he would find the worst qualities in those he had to meet. Why should he once again walk into the slime when there was so much goodness and kindliness to be found?

But of course he drove on. Curiosity, if nothing more, was sufficient temptation. Why had Millicent Griggs died? Why above all had she been buried in that open grave when the murderer could have escaped at once? Where was she murdered? These were questions enough for the moment without even considering the foremost and final one—who had killed her?

3

THE first person he interviewed in Gladhurst confirmed his feeling of vague repugnance at the case, for he realized almost at once that Naomi Chester was a very frightened young woman. Carolus hated to see fear in any human being, it was to him as embarrassing as nudity. Naomi did her best to conceal what she felt but unsuccessfully.

She was a thin tall girl, a trifle sallow and anaemic-looking yet rather pretty in a thoughtful way. She looked as though she could get and keep anything she wanted by merely clinging to it. She sat opposite Carolus and moved her thin arms and long fingers as though she were about to play cats' cradles with them. Her brown eyes were watchfully, indeed fearfully, on Carolus.

"How did you get on with the late Miss Griggs?" asked Carolus in a friendly reassuring voice.

"Oh, all right," said Naomi at once.

Lie One, thought Carolus, remembering what Mrs Bobbin had told him.

"You liked her?"

"Well, I wasn't much gone on all that church business," said Naomi.

"Did she talk to you much about that?"

"No. Not about that, she didn't."

"Other things, perhaps?"

"I never had much to do with her," said Naomi sulkily.

The conviction was growing on Carolus that Naomi was not only frightened but had something to conceal.

"She didn't want to know a lot about your private life?"

Naomi gave a small bitter smile.

"You haven't any private life in a place like Gladhurst," she said. "Everyone knows your business."

"But not everyone discusses it in front of you. Did Miss Griggs?"

"No!" said Naomi loudly and twined her fingers.

"Coming to the Thursday of her death. What time did you get here in the morning?"

"Nine. As usual."

"And leave?"

"I've gone over all this with the police. About half-past three."

"Was that your usual time?"

"I hadn't got one, really."

"I understand you normally left at about two-thirty."

Naomi was growing perceptibly more uncomfortable.

"When I can I do. It's often later."

"And that day it was later?"

"A bit, yes."

"Why?"

"I don't know."

"Why?"

"No reason. I just hadn't finished my work."

"Surely you'd washed up the lunch things?"

"Yes. Before Miss Flora left."

"Then what kept you?"

"Nothing. I was just running about finishing."

"Were you talking to Miss Griggs?"

"No. She was resting."

"Where?"

"Where she usually rested. In the drawing-room."

"You didn't go in there?"

"No."

"I should like to clear this up, you know. I know enough about housework to know that you'd have got all your rooms done in the morning so that after you'd washed up and put things away and just done the last oddments you could get off. You must have finished the washing-up at half-past two because Miss Flora caught the 2.40 bus. What did you do for another hour?"

"I don't know now. I was busy."

"Where?"

"Nowhere special. There were things to be done."

Carolus decided to use one of his diversions which so often brought out the truth.

"The drawing-room where Miss Griggs was resting is on the ground floor, isn't it? It has French windows?"

"Yes."

Naomi was staring at him now with a fixed melancholy.

"Were you near enough to hear if anyone had entered and talked to her there?"

"Oh yes. No one did that."

"Then where were you?"

24

"As a matter of fact I found I'd forgotten to do my hall."

"That's the central room of the house?"

"Yes. They don't like it being called the lounge. It's the hall."

"Wouldn't that be the first room you'd do?"

"No. The last. After I'd done those round it. Yes, I remember what it was kept me now. I found I'd forgotten it in the morning."

"Does it take an hour?"

"Oh yes. With all the staircase and that."

"I see. And all this time you heard and saw nothing of Miss Griggs?"

"No. When I looked in before leaving she was asleep."

"How was she lying?"

"On her back on the big settee with a lot of cushions under her head."

"Was there much light?"

"No. Not much. She always pulled the blinds before going to sleep."

"But you could see her face?"

"Only just."

"Where did you go from there?"

It was quite evident to Carolus that this was a new one. Whatever the police had asked Naomi they had stopped at the point of her leaving the house.

"Home," she said.

"You live with your mother?"

"Yes."

"Just the two of you?"

"S'right."

"Was she in when you got home?"

"No. She was at work. She's the head cook at Highcliff House."

"Who lives there?"

"It's a private nursing home. Just up the road. Mum's got a good job there."

"Didn't you ever think of working with her there?"

"I did only it upset me. All those poor things. So I went to work for these three. There wasn't the strain."

"You still haven't told me where you went that afternoon."

"Why? What's it to do with it? You're trying to find out who killed Miss Griggs, not worry about what I do in my own time."

"What time did you meet Grey?"

"Who said I met him that day?"

"Really, you are being rather silly, you know. You seem to want to make me think you had something to do with the death of Miss Griggs. I'll tell you frankly that I believe you know something you're afraid to tell. I can't see why you should be so evasive otherwise. Now don't start crying."

"I'm not crying," said Naomi unconvincingly. "Only you keep on at me with questions which have nothing to do with it."

"If they have nothing to do with it, why not answer them?"

"What is it you want to know?"

"What time you met Grey."

"He got off early that afternoon. He came home about four."

"To your home?"

"Yes, for a minute. Then he went off to see Estelle. That's his daughter. She's only two. Then he got changed and came back here to pick me up. Then we went off to the pictures."

"By bus?"

"No. Laddie, that's Laddie Grey, everyone calls him that, has got a motor-bike and side-car. We went to Burley in that."

"What is Grey's job?"

"He's on the building. Only there's not much doing this month."

"That's why he was able to get off early that afternoon?"

"I suppose so."

"Where was he working?"

"At Commander Fyfe's, I believe. Painting a room."

"How do you think Miss Griggs was killed?"

"Me? Oh I think the same as everyone else. Knocked on the head and robbed."

"On her way to the church?"

"I suppose so."

"You don't see anything difficult to believe about a woman leaving her afternoon snooze by a warm fire and walking through a dark afternoon to clean brass in an empty church?"

"Not with her I don't. She was church mad."

"You don't think she could have been killed anywhere but in the churchyard?"

"Well, it would be a bit risky in the road. Where else could she have been killed?"

"Anywhere. Here for instance."

Naomi goggled.

"In this house?"

"Why not?"

"I should have heard it."

"But after you had gone?"

"Of course I don't know what may have happened then."

"No. Did you come back that day?"

"Me? Come back? Whatever for?"

"You might have forgotten something."

"No. I never came back."

"You have your key?"

"Of the back door, yes."

"When did you hear about Miss Griggs's death?"

"Next morning. While I was at work. Slatt, the village policeman, came to see Mrs Bobbin and told her."

"You knew she was missing?"

"Only when I got to work. Miss Flora told me."

"When you left the house that afternoon did you walk home?"

27

"Yes. Of course."

"I wondered whether you had a bicycle," said Carolus mildly.

"No. I always walk."

"How far did you have to go? "

"About half a mile. Beyond the church."

"Whom did you pass on the way home? "

"No one. Why? "

"I quite understand that Gladhurst is a quiet little place, but surely between half past three and four on a fine weekday afternoon you'd have met someone? "

"Not that I remember I didn't."

"Please try to remember. It may be quite important."

"I think I saw the Reverend Slipper. That's the curate. He was just nipping into Jevonses the grocers. I don't know whether he saw me."

"No one else? "

"Not to my recollection."

"You didn't call anywhere? "

"Don't think so."

Carolus handed Naomi his cigarette-case and lit both cigarettes.

"Look here," he said, "won't you take my advice? I don't know *why* you're holding something back or who has persuaded you to, but whatever it is it's fatal not to be open in a case like this."

This time Naomi began to cry in earnest.

"I daresay you've been through a lot," said Carolus sympathetically, "but I'm afraid you'll have a good deal more unless you tell the truth. Why don't you? "

"There's nothing," blurted out Naomi between her sobs. "I've told you all I know."

"All right," said Carolus. "Have it your own way. Only if you decide to be sensible get hold of me or the police at once. Don't tell anyone else you're going to tell the truth. Really. You can phone me at the number I'm writing down or go to the police. But for heaven's sake don't hesitate."

28

Carolus saw her staring fixedly at him through tearful eyes. But she asked no question and in a moment went still sobbing from the room.

"I *knew* it would be a beastly case," he reflected.

A few minutes later Mrs Bobbin came into the room.

"You've made the girl cry," she said.

"I'm afraid she'll cry a good deal more before the case is over unless she decides to speak the truth. She knows something which she is determined not to reveal."

"But why?"

"I don't know. I shall in time. And she lies."

"What about?"

"I wanted to know what she did between 2.30 when your sister Flora left for Burley and 3.30 when, she says, she started out for home."

"What does she say she did?"

"Forgot to clean the hall in the morning. Remembered it and did it. Your sister Millicent meanwhile was sleeping in the drawing-room."

"What's wrong with that?"

"A woman doesn't *forget* to do the principal room of a house. And if by some freak she did she wouldn't spend an hour on it when it was time for her to go home."

"But the hall was done that day, very thoroughly. I remember noticing the smell of furniture polish when I came in. I congratulated Naomi on it next morning before we knew anything about Millicent. She said 'Yes, I did it last thing before going home'. So it doesn't sound as though she was lying at all."

"Then she told me she got on quite well with your sister Millicent though she never had much to do with her. After what you told me yesterday I knew that wasn't true."

"Well, she certainly did not get on with Milly as well as with Flora and me but then few people did. She probably *did* see less of her than of us."

"These are not perhaps very important. But I know that girl is hiding something and if you have any influence with her I hope you'll use it to persuade her to tell the truth."

"You're very sure of yourself, Mr Deene."

"When do you think I could meet your sister, Miss Flora?" asked Carolus.

"Tomorrow or the next time you come. She's not up to it today. It has been a severe shock to her."

"I quite understand. I have plenty of work to do. Tell me, how was your sister dressed when she was found?"

Mrs Bobbin looked at Carolus sharply.

"Exactly the clothes she was wearing when Flora left except for her fur coat."

"What about shoes?"

"Oh, she had changed those, of course. She had on a strong pair of walking shoes."

"She did not wear galoshes, of any sort? You must forgive my being old-fashioned enough to call them galoshes."

"She did, yes."

"Always, in winter?"

"Nearly always."

"And she wasn't wearing them?"

"No. Not that day. It was dry."

"Are they still in her room?"

"I suppose so."

"May I see them?"

"If Naomi hasn't gone." She went to the door. "Naomi!" she called rather stridently.

When the girl appeared Carolus saw that she had repaired her face and was looking more self-confident.

"Naomi," said Mrs Bobbin, "where are Miss Millicent's rubber shoes?"

"Her overshoes, you mean?" asked Naomi watchfully.

"Wasn't she wearing them?"

"I believe not."

"I'll see," said Naomi.

When she returned she said simply that they were nowhere to be found.

"Perhaps if she had not got them on when she was found she left them in the church?" suggested Naomi.

"Then surely Mrs Rumble would have come on them?" said Mrs Bobbin.

"Well, you know what *she* is," said Naomi meaningly.

"Yes," admitted Mrs Bobbin.

"You mean," said Carolus, "that your sister probably wore her galoshes and took them off while she was in the church?"

"It seems possible."

"Then either she forgot them when she left or else something happened to her while she was still in the building?"

"If Mrs Rumble found them there, yes."

"I shall have to see her tomorrow, then. Would your sister have taken anything with her from here if she went to clean brass in the church?"

"No. The things she used were kept in a cupboard in the vestry."

"Mrs Rumble will know if they had been disturbed?"

"Most unlikely. She had nothing to do with the brass."

"She lives near the church?"

"Just opposite."

"Well, thank you, Mrs Bobbin. I shan't have to trouble you again, I hope, though I would like to see Miss Flora as soon as possible."

"Have a cup of tea before you go? You run along, Naomi. I'll get it myself."

Half an hour later Carolus left the house and walked towards the church. It would be too late, he decided, to see much of the building but it was at about this time, according to Naomi's and Mrs Bobbin's conjectures, that Millicent Griggs would have taken this way nine days ago.

He could make out the tall shape of the square tower which stood apart from the village. Beside it was a fair-sized house which he took to be the vicarage and a small cottage which was probably Rumble's.

31

As he stood there a woman's figure approached him from the direction of the church and cottage.

"Good-night, Naomi," he said as the tall girl passed.

"Oh! Oh, good-night."

"Been to see Mrs Rumble?" asked Carolus.

"No! What? I was just . . . Why do you . . . Oh, leave me alone. I've told you everything. Why do you keep on?"

"I just said good-night," said Carolus. "Don't forget when you do want to tell the truth. . . ."

But Naomi was gone.

4

THAT evening Carolus paid his first visit to the Black Horse. He found it fairly crowded and after a while wondered what recommended it. Most pubs have something in their favour, something with which to enter the more or less bitter competition with their fellows. Where all have grown so stereotyped, each has to find a way faintly to distinguish it from the rest. So one will have a waggish, or a generous or a popular landlord, another a personable landlord's wife or daughter; in another there will always be a bright warm fire while yet another has beer from a brewery whose advertising has been successful in making men believe its beer is different from and better than the rest. In one there will be good darts, yet another is supposed to give a larger than ordinary measure of spirits. Yet all, being brewery-owned, licensing-hours-observing, well-regulated, standardized swilling-houses for standardized products at standardized prices, have lost all character, and in a few years their customers will be as standardized as they are. English pubs have ceased to differ one from another except superficially, their signs, their furniture, the way in which their antiquity has been restored may vary slightly, but there it ends.

·What made the gathering in the Black Horse choose it from among the three in the village? Not the landlord, surely, for a more dull and surly-looking man than George Larkin it would be hard to find. He stood back from his counter and said "Eh?" whenever anyone shouted for a drink. His most effusive welcome was a sudden small nod. It may have been the beer which attracted customers, but as there were several complaints about it that evening it seemed scarcely likely.

Then Carolus decided not to be carping. Perhaps the beer was better than it seemed. Perhaps George Larkin had a heart of gold.

> . . . *Folks of a surly tapster tell,*
> *And daub his visage with the smoke of Hell;*
> . . . *He's a Good Fellow, and 'twill all be well.*

Well, he might be, but Carolus, quietly sipping a Scotch and soda from a not too transparent glass still wondered at the inn's prosperity.

As the evening wore on he thought he found an explanation for it. Her name was Flo. She was a laughing buxom woman in her thirties who seemed to be everyone's friend. It was a tribute to her good nature that she was referred to as "old Flo". Of her it was said—"Flo doesn't mind", and that, in all its implications, was the secret of her popularity.

She was evidently a nightly customer and her jolly laugh, which doubled her plump body and brought tears to her eyes, could be heard at the end of each smutty story which Flo, quite evidently, "didn't mind". Was she, Carolus wondered in good old English phraseology, the village whore? No. She just didn't mind.

Carolus found himself being addressed by a small, mild, informative man.

"I come from what they call Hellfire Corner," he said

33

surprisingly. "Well, it's a name they give. It's only like a building estate really. There are one or two rough lots up there, though. Old Slatt, that's the copper, doesn't come up there more than he has to. I don't blame him. The last time he was nosing round someone dropped his bicycle down an old well there. He never did find out who did it and of course it made him look very silly with the Inspector. But there you are. Those that will keep hanging round at closing time what do you expect?"

Carolus recognized the question as rhetorical, bought two more drinks and settled down to listen.

His friend indicated a small stocky man with a flat face and a ready grin.

"That's Rumble," he said. "Sexton and verger!"

"He looks very cheerful for a sexton and verger."

"He *is* very cheerful. Why shouldn't he be? He enjoys his work, does Rumble. Very thorough he is. Well, you have to be with his job. His wife's just the opposite. Funny, isn't it, how you get that? She's as sour and nasty-tempered as he's easy-going. You don't often see her in here. She works for Miss Vaillant at the Old Vicarage."

"Is that the big house opposite the church?"

"Yes. The vicar's had to let it. He lives in a smaller place. Miss Vaillant's a character."

"In what way?"

"Queer old stick, she is. Well, not so old. Plenty of money, mind. Ah, here's Mrs Chester. I thought she'd be in. She's in charge of the kitchens up at Highcliff House. That's a big place for invalids. Sort of nursing home. You know, rich people who can afford it. Mrs Chester's worked there for years. She's a good sort. You ought to hear her and Flo if they get together. Laugh? Well, you *would* laugh. The things they come out with. Flo doesn't mind."

"That's a good thing, anyway."

"Old George Larkin takes no notice. I often wonder if he hears half the time. His son's a bit better than what he is but they're both pretty quiet."

34

"So I've noticed."

The younger Larkin had in fact joined his father behind the bar and seemed just as remote and discontented as the landlord.

Carolus found himself vigorously nudged by his informative new acquaintance.

"This is a real character, just come in," he said. "Mugger, his name is. Lives a few doors from me."

"What does he do for a living?"

"That's just it. Anyone would be hard put to it to say. Odd jobs here and there. Could be a wonderful gardener if he took the trouble. Now'n again he does a bit. Gives them a hand round at the Swan when they're busy. Goes in for keeping rabbits and pigeons and I don't know what. Breeds ferrets. Chickens, turkeys, anything like that. You ought to see his place. You wouldn't think it to look at him, would you?"

Without knowing quite what 'it' was, Carolus wouldn't. Mugger was a tall ginger-haired man, rather stern and serious in expression.

"Proper old fox, he is," went on the little man. "He doesn't half give old Slatt a time. Does it to pull his leg. Last winter Slatt caught him with a sack full of rabbits in a wood belonging to Commander Fyfe. Thought he'd got him at last, he did, and took him down to the police station to send him over to Burley. Old Mugger never said a word and when Slatt got on the phone to Commander Fyfe he found he'd given him permission to be there to keep the rabbits down."

"It seems to be a lively village," said Carolus.

"Of course this murder's upset things a bit. Scared a lot of people to think that such a thing could happen. Well, it's not very nice, is it? An old lady like that. They say the back of her head was smashed in something cruel. Makes you think."

"It does."

"She was a great churchgoer, Miss Griggs was. And her sister. Well, it's a place for churchgoing. I'm a bellringer myself. Only a lot have fallen off lately because of the larks this Miss Vaillant persuades the vicar to get up to. Wants him to start incense and she's got him dressed up like I don't know what with lace all over him. It doesn't do in a place like this. Miss Griggs was very much against it. I don't understand it myself but my wife says all that bobbing up and down and bowing and scraping is nothing less than roaming Catholic. There's talk of them starting idols next so I don't know what we are coming to! "

"Idols?"

"Well, images, then. It seems this Miss Vaillant brought one home from Italy and wanted it put in the church. Miss Griggs said if it went in she'd never come again and Miss Vaillant said if it didn't she wouldn't, so there you are. The poor vicar didn't know which way to turn. But they made it up somehow, because about a week before Miss Griggs died she started going to tea with Miss Vaillant. From what I hear she went twice in a week. It seems they came to terms. I never did hear what they arranged but Rumble heard from his wife that they got quite friendly all of a sudden. You don't know where you are with people like that, do you?"

"I don't."

"That's what poor old Chilling used to say. . . ."

"Chilling?"

"Bert Chilling. Just Passed On. It was in his grave as you remember that they'd put the body. He was a very nice chap, old Chilling. Used to come in here of an evening and very often ask you to have one. Can't say fairer than that, can I? Well, he was in the choir. Had been for years. And when this Miss Vaillant started these larks with the vicar and most of them were against it, old Chilling surprised them all. 'You give 'em plenty of it, Mr Waddell!' he used to say. 'Livens things up,' he told them. 'I like to see it', he said. 'Candles and vestments —the lot. I don't know why you don't put in confession boxes and be done with it.' Of course this came to Miss

Griggs's ears and she nearly passed out on the spot. But Miss Vaillant was ever so pleased. So there he was till suddenly he heard, on his deathbed as it turned out, that they'd made friends again. I shouldn't be surprised but what it Hastened his End. The shock of it, I mean. But you never know what to think, do you?"

"Not always," admitted Carolus and refilled their glasses.

"Lovibond's my name," admitted the small man rather coyly. "Fred Lovibond. I've got a little electrical business here. I was going to tȅll you how I came to have that. . . ."

"No, you weren't," said Carolus gently, "you were going to tell me the name of that young chap in the corner."

"That? That's Laddie Grey. Used to help Rumble in the churchyard in the old days. His wife's been Shut Up, poor chap. About this business of mine. . . ."

"I thought you were going to tell me about the murder of Miss Griggs."

"Oh well, that. That was a funny business. Right from the start I said it was a funny business. I mean, where was she going at that time of the night?"

"What time of the night?" asked Carolus.

"When she was done for. It can't have been in plain daylight can it? I mean, it would call attention."

"But it's dark by four."

"All right. But where was she going after four? It's all very well but I don't see anyone going into a cold church at that time. And where else could it have been? No one's seen her, don't forget."

"Then what do you think happened, Mr Lovibond?"

"Oh, I couldn't say. It doesn't bear thinking about really, does it? I mean it could have been anyone, almost. It came out at the inquest that it might have been a woman just as well as a man. I think myself it must have been a stranger. I can't see anyone in Gladhurst doing it. I suppose we shall know in good time. I hear they've got all the biggest policemen on it. Can't let anything like

37

that go past, can they? Old Slatt's been going round like a dog with two tails. '*We* shall probably be making an arrest shortly,' he says. Makes you laugh, doesn't it? "

"I don't know Slatt," said Carolus.

"You'll find him out in the square now. Always out there in the evening, waiting for ten o'clock. He likes to have a chat while he's standing there looking at his watch for closing time. He talks quick enough. It's a job to stop him talking."

Carolus found him without difficulty, a long-faced, solemn man who looked suspiciously at the world as though he feared it was going to burst into an explosion of laughter at the sight of him.

Carolus addressed him cheerfully.

"You're the Gladhurst policeman, aren't you? "

"Police *Officer*," said Slatt in a gloomy voice. " P'raps you wasn't aware that the status has been changed? Police Officer, please."

"Good evening, Police Officer," said Carolus obligingly. " Nice evening for murders."

"I take it you're a stranger here," said Slatt. "Otherwise you wouldn't make jokes of that sort."

A motor-bike sped by and immediately the whole bearing of Slatt changed. He ceased to be a lethargic individual leaning on a bicycle and became a crouching lion.

"See the way they go by? " he said. " It's disgraceful, really it is. You can't do anything about it either. We've got half a dozen or more in the village itself and they come through all the time."

"What's wrong with them? "

"Wrong with them? They're dangerous, smelly, noisy and you never know what the young people who ride on them are up to."

"Does it matter? "

"Of course it matters. You can't have people doing what they like. These motor-bikes bring trouble all round. We're always getting complaints. When we're busy with

38

something like this murder we don't want trouble with motor-bikes, do we? If I had my way. . . ."

"You will, I expect, before long. Everything points to it anyway. But how do motor-bikes add to the confusion of the murder? "

"Because part of the investigation I carried out concerned their movements on that day. It was thought necessary to know which of them were where at the time of the crime. How was I to discover that with them flying round like wasps? There's young Bill Larkin the son of this House opposite got one and the Reverend Slipper the curate just bought one for running about on. Then Laddie Grey, he's had one for a long time and Albert Chilling whose father died the other day and two or three more. What they've got up at Hellfire Corner no one knows—half of them not insured I daresay. But I can't be everywhere at once, can I? "

"I suppose not."

"As soon as I've stopped one and given him a warning for speeding there's another I find with his licence out of date. What am I to do? It's the same with the pubs. If I'm here at ten o'clock when they close I can't be outside the Swan as well and I heard it was nearly five past before they were all out of there the other night. That's only the half of it. There's swedes been missing from a pile beside the road to Burley and all the poaching to think of. I have to have eyes at the back of my head."

"Poaching? " prodded Carolus.

"We've one or two really bad characters round here," said Slatt darkly.

"Oh? ' A policeman's lot is not a happy one ', I gather."

"A police *officer*."

"I beg your pardon. ' A police officer's lot is not a happy one ', I should say."

"No. It's very difficult sometimes. Do you live here? "

"No."

"Staying in the village? "

"No."

39

" Is that your car over there? "

" Yes."

" Isn't that what you call a Bentley Continental? "

" It is."

" You seem interested in what goes on here."

" I am. Particularly murder."

" That's a matter I can't discuss. It would never do for a police officer."

" No. Of course not. Besides, I'm a stranger."

" Yes," said Slatt suspiciously. " And we don't get many strangers in Gladhurst."

" None on the day of the murder, I understand? "

" Not so far as we're aware. And we've covered it pretty thoroughly. Bus, train, roads, shops, private houses. No one saw anyone they didn't know."

" It must be very difficult for you. A dark afternoon, motor-bicycles and no strangers. You don't even know the time it happened, I'm told."

" Not to the minute, we don't."

" You should know that. They say ' if you want to know the time ask a policeman '."

" Police officer," corrected Slatt.

" Of course. ' If you want to know the time, ask a police officer '."

" That's better," said Slatt. " No, we don't know the exact time but if you had the experience of these cases that I have you'd know that time is not the all-important factor. That's an idea put about by these detective writers." He paused to look at his watch. " Still four minutes to go," he said.

Carolus smiled.

" So time has its importance in matters of the licensing laws? "

" That's another matter. It would never do to let people hang about in pubs half the night, would it? What would happen to their work next day, do you think? "

" I should have thought that the time he goes to bed might have been a man's own affair."

40

"His *own* affair?" said Slatt, horrified. "Whatever do you think would happen to the country if we let people do what they liked? I'm surprised at a man like you suggesting such a thing."

"Anarchic, you think?"

"Worse than that. Why very soon we'd have them up at all hours dancing and singing and I don't know what. How would you expect me to keep law and order then, I should like to know."

"Do you sleep well?" asked Carolus.

"No, I don't," said Slatt. "That's my trouble."

"I thought it might be. Makes me think of Kipling—

> *Over the edge of the purple down,*
> *Where the single lamplight gleams,*
> *Know ye the road to the Merciful Town*
> *That is hard by the Sea of Dreams—*
> *Where the poor may lay their wrongs away,*
> *And the sick may forget to weep?*
> *But we—pity us! Oh, pity us!*
> *We wakeful; ah, pity us!—*
> *We must go back with Policeman Day—*
> *Back from the City of Sleep!"*

"Police *officer*," Slatt reminded him.

"Of course—

> *We must go back with Police Officer Day*
> *Back from the City of Sleep."*

"Time they was out," said Slatt and strode across to the Black Horse.

5

WHEN Carolus next came to Gladhurst he decided to act on Mrs Bobbin's assurance that he would find it a parish matter. He asked for the vicarage and was directed to a small new semi-detached villa. The door was opened by a young woman with bright professional cheerfulness, like that of a hospital nurse.

"Yes, my father's at home," she beamed. "Come in if you can squeeze your way along this passage. Mrs Bobbin told us to expect you. Father's in here."

Mr Waddell was as bright and beaming as his daughter, a bald, round, obliging sort of man.

"De-lighted," he said. "De-lighted, my dear fellow. Anything I can tell you is at your disposal. I shall be only too happy." Suddenly he looked serious. "Unless of course it conflicts with my duty to the police."

Carolus, not yet used to the vicar's facility for discovering the horns of a dilemma and being tossed from one to the other, said—"I don't think so."

"I've always understood that private detectives and CID men were at loggerheads," the vicar continued anxiously. "I shouldn't wish to find myself. . . ."

"No, no," said Carolus briskly. "What did you do that afternoon, Mr Waddell?"

The vicar recovered his jollity and gift for being all things to all men.

"Ah hum!" he beamed. "You're certainly not afraid of convention, Mr Deene. That, if I may use the expression, is an old one. What's more I think I can answer it pretty accurately. I lunched at home. My wife and daughter. Cottage pie, I remember. A little argument about whether it should be called Cottage or Shepherd's. My wife became quite impassioned about it. I found myself weighing the balance between them. I dislike dis-

42

agreement. We can't all hold the same opinions about everything but we needn't be dogmatic. A little sweet reasonableness here, a small compromise there and the world. . . ."

" You were telling me what you did that afternoon."

"Yes. Yes. I get carried away. I went to see my Church-warden. Commander Fyfe."

" Is he as keen as you are on agreement among people? "

"He has recently joined me in a little conspiracy which, until this sad event in the parish, we thought successful. Two good and sincere women—sincere each in her own manner—had been long in conflict. Miss Griggs might be described as evangelical in her views, Miss Vaillant held opposite opinions. Miss Vaillant wished me to introduce a form of ritual which Miss Griggs considered out of keeping . . . inappropriate . . . not in accordance with her conception of the Church of England. In a word, Miss Vaillant was High Church, Miss Griggs, Low."

"And you? "

" Oh, Broad. Broad. I could not subscribe to some of the more exuberant notions of Miss Vaillant and felt her use of the word 'Mass' was open to misinterpretation. On the other hand I felt that Miss Griggs, sincere though she was, might wish to deprive our fine old church of some of its grandeur."

" So how did you manage the situation? "

"Well, I had liturgical colours, you know, and we turned to the East for the Creed. I had to draw the line at holy water but I allowed those of the choir who wished it to make the sign of the cross. I had six candlesticks on the altar but kept a plain cross and felt bound to refuse the large crucifix presented by Miss Vaillant. We used the term Sung Eucharist but I wouldn't allow Matins to be ousted from the hour of eleven o'clock. As for Confessions, I expressed myself willing to hear them but chiefly in cases of illness. I agreed rather reluctantly to the choir wearing the lace cottas which Miss Vaillant presented after their surplices were worn out but I would

43

not go so far as scarlet cassocks. Recently, after much careful consideration of the subject, I took the important step of wearing vestments at Sung Eucharist though not at the Early Morning Communion Service which the Misses Griggs attended. I would not allow incense but we were considering a side chapel."

" It all sounds very sensible," said Carolus.

" But of course the parties at both extremes were dissatisfied. It is so often the way. I had distressing scenes with Miss Vaillant when she wished to prevail on me to wear a biretta and Miss Griggs refused to attend the church on one occasion until I had removed a Paschal Light. But recently, after years of moving among these discordances, I seemed to perceive a ray of light. With the aid of my Churchwarden, splendid chap, we at least induced the two ladies to be on speaking terms. It appears that an agreement was reached that when together they should discuss everything except religion, the church, our services. It seemed to work so well that Miss Griggs actually went to Miss Vaillant's home on two occasions recently. Then came this dreadful murder to throw a shadow over all."

" Thank you for those interesting details," said Carolus. " Now may I bring you back to the afternoon of the tragedy."

" I was saying I walked round to Commander Fyfe's pleasant home, The Fairway. Perhaps you know Commander Fyfe? "

" Not yet."

" An excellent fellow. A really grand chap. But apt— how shall I put it?—to see mystery, even intrigue, where none is noticeable to others. He reads newspapers which are inclined to stress the more sensational aspects of national life. But the best of men. We discussed the hopeful situation that had risen between the two ladies and one or two other parish matters. An unfortunate rift has arisen between our organist-choirmaster, Mr Waygooze and my enthusiastic curate Peter Slipper. Slipper's splendid with boys. Scouts, Boys' Club, Camping, splendid. Waygooze naturally wants them for the choir and the two enthusiasms clash. I see Waygooze's point of view, of course, and I support Slipper in his endeavours. I find myself . . ."

"Just so. That afternoon?"

"I took a cup of tea with Commander and Mrs Fyfe, then decided to call at the church on my way home."

"May I be impertinent enough to ask why?"

"Certainly, my dear chap. Cer-tainly. No impertinence at all. It is a custom of mine. From time to time I spend a while there in contemplation. We do not Reserve, of course, but the church is something more than a mere meeting-place. My verger Rumble locks it at night. Most conscientious, Rumble. A loyal employee. He has a very happy disposition in spite of his domestic trouble. His wife, you know. They don't Get On. Most unfortunate. How many times have I tried to pour oil on those troubled waters? Mrs Rumble works for Miss Vaillant and is apt to take her view of the little controversy which has disturbed my flock. Rumble does a certain amount of gardening at Crossways when he has time. Perhaps because of that he takes the view so ardently held by the Misses Griggs. Frankly I do not know which, if either, was to blame. On the one hand Rumble seems to have a happy disposition, on the other it is not always the more bitter ones who are responsible for quarrels."

"You were saying that you went to the church?"

"Yes. At about five o'clock."

"That would mean that its lights were on and could be seen from outside?"

"Yes. When I arrived the church was in darkness. I switched on the main light over the chancel."

"Was there anything unusual or out-of-place?"

"Not that I observed. All seemed quite as it should be. Mrs Rumble keeps the church in order. I saw nothing to criticize though I was not that moment looking for anything."

45

"Was there any sign of the brass having been recently cleaned?"

"Now there you have me," said the vicar. "I did not notice the brass."

"Not even the lectern?"

"No. The lectern is in the form of a magnificent brass eagle with outspread wings. It was a gift from the father of the Misses Griggs and Mrs Bobbin before I had the living. You may know the kind of thing?"

"I do indeed."

"I certainly did not notice that afternoon if it had been recently polished."

"Pity. Did you happen to see a pair of galoshes near the door?"

"Galoshes?" repeated the vicar.

"Rubber overshoes."

"Near the door?"

"Yes, Mr Waddell. Near the door."

"No. That would be most unusual."

"But it was dark when you arrived? You could have passed them?"

"I think not. The switches for all the lights are at the West end of the church."

"Still, you can't be certain?"

"No. I can't be certain."

"You see, Mr Waddell, there is a suggestion that Millicent Griggs went to the church that afternoon to clean her brass. She may have been murdered on the way to the church, or coming away from it, or even *in* it, for all we know."

"Terrible. Terrible."

"So anything you could tell me which would suggest that she had been there, or had not been there. . . ."

"I hardly know what to say. On the one hand all seemed so peaceful yet on the other I suppose that shortly before or after my visit. . . . Terrible. My wife would like you to take a cup of tea with us."

"I shall be delighted. You saw nothing?"

46

"Nothing unusual, no."

"And heard nothing?"

"Not in the church. Not at that time."

"Then?"

"After returning here I set out to call on Miss Vaillant. Miss Vaillant, as you may know, occupies the Old Vicarage just opposite the church. I couldn't possibly afford to keep it up and got permission to let it while we have moved into these more modest quarters. It was past six when I approached Miss Vaillant's house. The church was, of course, in darkness. The village seemed quiet. A dark peaceful night. Then, just before I rang the bell, I heard the sound of a motor-bike engine starting up."

"Where?"

"It *sounded* as though it came from the lane behind the church."

"Was that very unusual?"

"Well, no. That lane is used, I gather, by the young people of the village. Harmless, I'm sure . . . I suppose . . . I hope. Our village policeman seems perturbed about it. He explained to me that once the young folk imagine they can do what they want. . . ."

"Yes, he gave me his views on public morality. So why did you particularly notice that motor-cycle being started?"

"I hardly know. But I did notice it."

The cheerful daughter came to the door.

"Tea's ready," she said, and Carolus found himself following her to a small drawing-room where Mrs Waddell was already seated behind a silver tray. "A lean and hungry-looking woman who seems thoroughly dissatisfied with life" was Mrs Bobbin's description of her and it fitted. She did not look too pleased at the inclusion of Carolus in the party. She gave him a toothy and unwilling smile and after a minute or two spoke to him.

"I may as well tell you, Mr Deene, that I was against

47

my husband giving you any information in this matter at all. It seems to me wholly a police affair."

"You think the police will discover the murderer, Mrs Waddell?"

"I daresay. I'm not much interested. But I see no reason to assist a private detective. Milk and sugar?"

"Please. I hope the police are successful," said Carolus and added mischievously—"It would be disgraceful if a kind, generous and devout old lady could . . ."

The thin face of Agatha Waddell had turned scarlet.

"Is that the impression you have been given about the late Millicent Griggs?" she asked.

"Agatha, my dear . . ." protested the vicar.

"Now, mother," said his daughter.

"I don't know who can have told you that," said Agatha Waddell. "Millicent Griggs was kind to no one but herself, she was generous only to gain her own ends and as for her devoutness she was the most hypocritical, narrow-minded. . . ."

"Agatha, my dear, what *will* Mr Deene think of us?"

"I don't care what he thinks. If he's fool enough to believe that Millicent Griggs was kind. . . ."

"You must forgive my wife's strong feelings, Mr Deene. She had her difficulties with the late Miss Griggs, as we all had."

"Perhaps you were of the other faction, Mrs Waddell?" suggested Carolus.

"Grazia Vaillant's? Certainly not. A gushing insincere woman."

"My dear, we must be charitable in our judgments."

"There's a limit to charity. I've seen my husband's life here made a purgatory by these two self-centred, bigoted women."

"Aren't you somewhat overstating the case, dear? They have been most generous."

"When it suited them. More tea, Mr Deene? I wonder how *you* would like being a vicar's wife in a small country parish."

"I'm sure I should find it a most difficult transformation," said Carolus, pacifically.

"Intrigue, suspicion, back-biting, jealousy the whole time."

"You are not suggesting that Millicent Griggs was murdered from sheer malice, are you?"

"I'm not suggesting anything. But there's enough malice in Gladhurst to murder fifty people."

"You alarm me."

"Millicent Griggs herself was capable of it."

"Really?"

"I know for a fact that she wrote to the Bishop."

"What about?"

"Prejudice again. Fortunately the Bishop knows my husband. He has been here to lunch. Otherwise it might have meant all sorts of difficulties for us. She said that my husband intended to ride into church on an ass on Palm Sunday."

"And didn't he?" asked Carolus who unfortunately knew very little about ritual.

"Certainly not. She even implied that there was something between my husband and Grazia Vaillant."

"And . . ." Carolus stopped himself in time. "And that was an obvious lie," he said.

"Of course. There was no limit to what that woman would say."

There was a long pause.

"I wonder whether just for the sake of form, Mrs Waddell, you will tell me how you spent that afternoon? I have to ask everyone that."

To Carolus's surprise she acceded without protest.

"I had my Mothers from four to six."

"Where?" said Carolus not revealing his ignorance of her meaning.

"At the Institute."

"Oh, I see. And afterwards?"

"I came home."

"And you, Miss Waddell?"

49

"Who? Me?" laughed Rosa Waddell. "I was out on my bike. Went over to Burley, as a matter of fact."

"For anything particular?"

"Not really. More for the run than anything."

"See anyone you knew?"

"No. Can't say I did. Why? Don't say I'm a suspect? I often felt like bashing Millicent Griggs but you surely don't think I actually did it?"

"I haven't got to the point of having suspects. I'm only just beginning to get a notion *where* it happened. I certainly don't pretend to guess when or through whom. Were you back before your mother?"

"Yes. I got my own tea. I was hungry, too. Then I settled down to a book. Thirkell. You know, goes on and on but you feel you have to find out what happens to the dreary people. Daddy popped in for a few minutes and rushed out again. Then mother arrived."

"You didn't notice any times?"

"I suppose daddy came around six and mother a good bit later."

"What do you call a good bit?"

"Well, it was about a quarter to seven when mummy turned up."

"Thank you, Miss Waddell. I think you said, Mr Waddell, that you called on Miss Vaillant after coming home?"

"I said I went to her house. I did so. In fact I had arranged to do on the previous morning."

"Did you stay long?"

The vicar beamed good-humouredly. "I didn't stay at all. I didn't enter. Miss Vaillant was out. I rang several times without result."

"That's interesting," said Carolus seriously.

"Yes," smiled the vicar, who seemed to think he had made a good remark, "Miss Vaillant was out."

6

MUCH though Carolus wanted to meet Grazia Vaillant he felt it more important to see the Rumbles, husband and wife separately. In piecing together his picture of events that afternoon, in fixing times and forming an idea of where the various inhabitants of Gladhurst were likely to have been, he needed to hear what the Rumbles would tell him.

Another fine clear day found Carolus over at Gladhurst, making for the churchyard, since he understood that at this time the sexton would be working there. As he approached he heard a cheerful voice singing *Rockin' Along in the Breeze*.

He found Rumble, who stopped singing and looked up with a grin.

"You're the one who is going to find out who did for her, aren't you?" he said.

"I hope so," returned Carolus briefly. Coming straight to the point, he said: "You found the body, I understand?"

It seemed that Rumble did not like this short cut across his reminiscences.

"I found the body," he said, "but *how* did I find it? How was it I came to disturb the grave waiting for Mr Chilling? How is it Miss Griggs isn't down there now and no one the wiser?"

"Ah!" said Carolus who from many cross-examinations had learnt the value of this long-drawn monosyllable in such contexts.

Rumble grinned.

"There's a lot to know about burying," he said. "And from what I hear we're not a patch on the ancient Egyptians. What do we do, when all's said and done? Make a box for 'em with brass fittings and drop it under six foot of soil. Well, not six foot really because the ground doesn't have to be dug more than six foot down. I always do mine seven. Seven to the inch. That's how I came to know Chilling's had been tinkered with. I dropped my tape down the evening before and said to old Mugger who was helping me, there you are, I said, that's seven foot to the inch so Chilling'll have the best part of six foot on top of him when he's in tomorrow. Next morning when I measured it, it was scarcely more than five. So I said to myself this is funny, I said, something peculiar's been going on here and I jumped in and started digging down again. It wasn't two minutes before I came on Miss Griggs."

Rumble smiled broadly.

"I suppose that was rather unnerving for you?"

"Well, you get used to anything like that in this job."

"Do you really?"

"I've never found what you might call a recent one before but I've come on old 'uns. Been there hundreds of years and not much left. It's not so bad as it was but my dad and grandad had the job here before me and I've heard it was a proper sardine tin before they enlarged the churchyard. There was vaults under the church cram-packed with coffins. You could smell it. Well, I think you can still, very often. Sort of musty smell. Outside in the old graveyard, which only went as far as that yew tree, they used to pop 'em in one on top of the other till they were only just under the surface. So it's not surprising that now'n again when I'm digging a new grave I come on something, is it?"

"I suppose not."

"Though of course not like this. She was lying on her back and the earth had been just shoved in over the top. It looked as though it might have been done in the dark. It was lucky I looked; otherwise she'd have been under old Chilling till Judgment Day and that would never have done, would it?"

"Never," agreed Carolus sternly. "What did you do when you found the body?"

"Nipped straight over to see the Reverend Waddell. Course, he was very upset. He got on to the police right away and I will say they weren't long in coming out. Then—you should have seen them. You've never seen such a pantomime in all your life. Every bit of ground was gone over inch by inch. They must have taken away a couple of hundredweight of soil. They was taking photographs and measuring up and examining the ground. But after all that, they said it was all right. We could go ahead burying Chilling that afternoon as arranged. That was a relief to everyone."

"Why?"

"Well, the expense. He'd been taken over to Worsley's the undertakers at Burley and was Lying there. It all costs money. And though I believe he's left his widow comfortable no one likes to see it wasted, do they? Besides it was all arranged for that afternoon. Reverend Waddell was going to bury him himself. It would have meant time wasted. But the police seemed to understand that. They said it was all right to go ahead. So we did and Chilling's down there on his own. Just the one bell, he had, and the organist without the choir. All very nice but nothing extravagant. You should have seen it when the Miss Griggs's father was buried. That *was* a funeral. You'd have thought it was royalty. Of course he'd been very good to the parish. Fiver for me every Christmas and fifty quid in the Easter Collection. Not to mention other things."

"Were you digging the grave on that Thursday afternoon?"

"That's right. Me'n Mugger."

"What time did you finish?"

"Must have been well before four. It was beginning to get dark and you know what time that happens. I daresay we'd finished and put our tools away by half-past three."

53

"Where did you put your tools? "

"In the furnace room."

"Is that locked? "

"No. No need in a place like this."

"So anyone can have used those tools to throw the earth over Miss Griggs's body? "

"I don't suppose anyone knew they were there. The police examined 'em all for finger prints and there was only mine on them."

"I see. What did you and Mugger do when you'd finished? "

"I went home. He lives over the other side of the village. He left me near my cottage and went on."

"While you were digging did anyone come to the churchyard? "

"Not while we were digging, they didn't."

"But afterwards? Did you meet anyone as you came away? "

Rumble looked somewhat perplexed.

"It doesn't seem worth mentioning," he said, "but as me'n Mugger left the churchyard we did happen to meet George Larkin and his son Bill."

"Where were they going? "

"They went into the churchyard."

"To the church? "

"I don't know. It was getting a bit dark and we wanted to get home."

"Were you surprised to see the Larkins? "

"I was a bit. George isn't much of a churchgoing man though he does come sometimes on Sunday mornings."

"Did you speak to them? "

"Just passed the time of day."

"They didn't say where they were going? "

"No. They never say much, as you'd know if you went to the Black Horse. Anyhow we didn't stop and ask questions."

"Have you ever seen them there before? "

"Can't say I have. But that's not to say they've never

been. No. I said good-night to George and Bill and went over to my home."

"Was there anyone at your home?"

"Do you mean my old woman? There was no one else to be at home. No. She hadn't come back from Vaillant's then. She came in about five. I remember that because she said there was a light on in the church. Not often she'll bother to speak. She's a funny-tempered woman, my wife. Still, she did say that afternoon, there's a light on over in the church. So I went out to look and she was right."

"What did you do about it?"

"I was just going over when I saw old Flo coming across." Rumble paused to laugh reminiscently. "You know Flo?"

"By sight."

"She's all right, is Flo. She's a good sport! Liked all round except by some of the wives. They hate her, some of them. Think their husbands are too friendly with her. Well, so they may be. Flo doesn't mind. Anyway, there she was. 'It's only Mr Waddell,' she said, 'I just saw him go in.' I asked her where she was going and she said wouldn't I like to know, then I heard my old woman coming so I shut the door to save trouble and argument."

"Quite."

"I didn't bother any more about the church till after I'd had my tea, then when I looked out the lights were off. So I walked over and locked up."

"Did you look round before doing so?"

"No. I didn't go in at all. There was nothing to go in for."

"You didn't meet anyone when you went across?"

"Not a soul."

"Nor hear anything?"

"Nothing unusual."

"Thanks, Rumble. You've been very helpful."

Rumble grinned.

"Going to try the old woman?"

55

"There are one or two things I want to ask her."
Rumble seemed amused at that.

"I wish you luck," he said darkly.

"I gather you don't approve of Miss Vaillant's religious views?"

"It's not that. It's the work it makes. Processions and that. She wants to start burning incense all over the place. It was Commander Fyfe who stopped that by asking what the Insurance people would say about it. I've got my job as verger without dressing up in lace and carrying a banner on a pole. Besides people don't like it. The collections have fallen off since she started persuading the Reverend Waddell. We don't get the weddings we did, either. Baptisms are down. And Confirmations are nowhere. It all means less for me and it's little enough as it is. There was a lot of trouble last Ash Wednesday when she wanted the vicar to start smudging everyone's faces with charcoal. Have you ever heard anything like it? Miss Griggs, the old lady that's been done for, asked if she wanted to turn us all into chimney sweeps. The Reverend Waddell didn't know what to do."

"What *did* he do?"

"Well, he did her and no one else. That was his way out of it. She walked about looking as though she'd been cleaning out the grate and forgotten to wash. She couldn't complain because she'd got what she wanted and Miss Griggs couldn't say much either because no one else had it. But they were like two tiger cats, those two. Never knew two women hate one another as they did and the vicar's wife hated the pair of them. Nice state of affairs."

"Very."

"You go across and see the old woman. She's at home now. But don't blame me if she won't let you in. She's very funny about things."

"I can only try," said Carolus.

"I hope you *do* find out who done it," chuckled Rumble. "Though with no disrespect I can't help smiling

56

when I think how cross the old lady would have been if she'd known she was going to be banged on the head. She was one to fly into a fit of temper anytime. Well, all three of them were—Mrs Bobbin perhaps most of the lot. I often think it is a village for that. There was the lady who's Gone and her two sisters, and my old woman who is as bad as any of them, and that Miss Vaillant, *she*'s got a temper too, and the vicar's wife and one or two more. Not old Flo, though. You never see her put out whatever happens. But Mugger's wife was another who flies off the handle at the least thing. You've never seen such tantrums as we have here. But it never bothers me. I just laugh."

"Very sensible. Tell me, since you worked for her you must have known something of Miss Millicent Griggs?"

"Want me to tell you straight?" Rumble did. "That's what she was. Mean with her sisters and everyone else. Always *right*, if you know what I mean. Do anyone a nasty turn. Not like that Miss Flora who is sincere in what she thinks."

"Thanks, Rumble."

"Well, I wish you luck with my old woman. Only if I see you flying down the road in a minute I shan't be surprised."

As Carolus left him he heard him singing blithely. *Hook, Line and Sinker* was the number he chose to volley among the gravestones.

Carolus decided that if he was to get any information from Mrs Rumble strategy would be necessary. He knocked loudly at the cottage door and when it was opened by a dishevelled and irritated woman with her mouth already open to abuse him he spoke before she could.

"I'm enquiring about a pair of galoshes," he said.

The effect was as startling as he hoped. The lower jaw dropped farther and the eyes searched his. Then Mrs Rumble looked quickly up and down the street and said, "Come inside quick and let me shut the door."

In a musty and cold front room she faced Carolus with a defensive expression.

"What galoshes?" she asked.

"Don't let's beat about the bush, Mrs Rumble. You know quite well what I mean."

"I've never Took anything in my life," she said. "Least of all out of the church."

"No?"

"Certainly not. I wouldn't if you was to pay me. Things left behind in the pews and that."

"What do you do with them?"

"If there was anything left behind I should take it to the vicar."

"Did you take the galoshes to the vicar?"

"I was going to. Soon as ever I had a minute."

"Did you tell him you'd found them?"

"Not yet, I haven't. I haven't had a chance to turn round."

"When did you find them?"

"Last Sunday morning. That's the day before yesterday."

"Where were they?"

"Pushed right underneath at the back of the church. They might have been there for weeks."

"You don't know to whom they belonged?"

"No. I don't. If I did I'd have run straight round with them. It's my belief they were left behind by some visitor a long while back."

"Wouldn't you have found them, in that case?"

"I might have if what I was paid for looking after the church was enough for me to be looking everywhere morning, noon and night, but it's not. I can't go washing and polishing on my hands and knees every day in every square inch of that yewje building, can I?"

"I suppose not. Did you do all the cleaning in the church?"

"All except the brass, I did. Miss Griggs liked to do that herself."

58

"Do you remember going over to the church on the morning when your husband found her body? The Friday morning, I mean."

"I'm not likely to forget it."

"Did you notice then whether the brass had been cleaned recently or not?"

"Not then, I didn't, but later in the day I did. I noticed it hadn't been done for a week or more and I thought, I suppose *that*'ll be expected of me now that Miss Griggs isn't any longer here to do it. Well, I can only do *so* much, I thought."

"You are quite sure no one had cleaned it or started to clean it on the previous afternoon?"

"Certainly Miss Griggs hadn't. She always started with the lectern which is a neagle with its wings holding up the Bible. Her father gave it to the church and she thought a lot of it. It was that I noticed that day. It was ever so tarnished all over."

"Thank you. That's very helpful."

"Are you from the police, then?" asked Mrs. Rumble.

"No. I'm just trying to find out who killed Miss Griggs."

"You don't need to say anything about those galoshes, do you? It might be thought bad of."

"Certainly not. But if I may suggest it, I think you should report finding them."

Mrs Rumble looked at him dubiously then seemed to take a momentous decision.

"I'd just put the kettle on when you knocked," she said.

Carolus waited.

"I don't know whether you'd like a cup of tea. Only you'd better come through to the kitchen where there's a fire."

Comfortably seated in what he supposed was Rumble's chair, Carolus prepared to ask more questions while the unprecedented affability of Mrs Rumble lasted.

"I understand you work for Miss Vaillant?"

59

" Well, I do, yes. I can't give all my time to the church and it helps."

"You share her religious views, I believe? "

" I wouldn't call it that. Only I do think it brightens things up to have a bit of colour and music instead of psalms, psalms, psalms all the time. I don't say I should want to go as far as what she would, especially when she came back from Spain last year and wanted to start teaching the choir to do a dance in the middle of the chancel. But if those Miss Griggses had their way it would be one long Bible meeting."

"You think Miss Vaillant sincere in what she wanted? "

"Well, if the truth were known . . . I don't know whether I ought to Speak . . ."

"Yes? "

" The truth is, she Drinks," whispered Mrs Rumble. "There. Truth will out. Secret, of course. No one ever had any idea about it except Forster's Stores over at Burley where she got the stuff and brought it away in her own car. Gin it was. She used to put lime juice in it to take the taste away. I wouldn't have known myself if I hadn't happened to have a key which fitted the cupboard and could see the bottle. But she wasn't the only one."

" She wasn't? "

" No. And this will surprise you. Old Miss Griggs Liked a Drop, too. What do you think brought them together right at the end? Miss Griggs went to see her twice after they hadn't been speaking for I don't know how long. The first time I met her coming out. All flushed up she was, besides I could smell her breath. Oh, I thought, so you Like a Drop, too, do you? They forgot all about their differences after that."

" You say Miss Vaillant kept her gin in a locked cupboard? "

" Yes. In her sitting-room. Only one bottle at a time. She'd rather have died than let anyone know about it. You know what she does with the empty bottles? It just shows you how cunning they are. There's an old well out-

60

side the backdoor. They say it's ever so old and goes down no one knows how deep. She'd fill the empties with water so that they'd sink, then drop them down and no one was to know any different."

"How did you come to be aware of it?"

"I saw her one night when I'd gone back for something. She never knew I saw her."

"Did she stick to one brand of gin?"

"Yes. Horseley's. You know the bottles? Kind of oval shaped."

"How do you know that?"

"Well, my nephew works over at Forster's Stores in Burley."

"You think she drank regularly?"

"No. I'm sure she didn't. It was only about once a week. When she couldn't resist it, I suppose. You know what secret drinkers are, don't you?"

"You don't think she was at all violent when she had been drinking?"

"I know very well she was. I've come in in the morning more than once and found things broken which could only have been on purpose."

"And you don't think her reconciliation with Miss Griggs went very deep?"

"No, I don't. They'd been at one another's throats too many years for that."

"How do you suppose, then, that they came to talk intimately enough for Miss Vaillant even to suggest a drink?"

"Well, when I took their tea in on Miss Griggs's first visit, I heard something. Miss Griggs had just noticed the tube of Minerval tablets which Miss Vaillant had. They're for sleeping, prescribed by Dr Pinton. 'Oh', she said, 'Dr Pinton gives you these, does he?' I make no doubt she took them, too. That may have set them talking."

Just then the back door opened and Rumble entered. If his wife had shown surprise when Carolus first appeared

61

Rumble was now dumbstruck at the scene which greeted him.

"What are you gaping for?" asked his wife. "Never seen a gentleman drink a cup of tea before?"

"Not in this kitchen, I haven't," said Rumble recovering himself.

"Well, you're seeing it now so take those filthy boots off and sit down and behave yourself."

Rumble gave his tolerant grin.

"I don't know how you managed it," he said to Carolus.

"Now don't Start," said Mrs Rumble. "Upon my soul I don't wish anyone any harm but I can't help thinking it's a pity there's not more Taken in this village. Rumble's never happy unless he's digging a grave."

"I thought he was always happy."

"That's just Appearances," said Mrs Rumble. "He's got to be out there measuring it up and getting it right or else he's not fit to live with. I *know*. I've seen him looking round wondering who the next will be."

"Any ideas on the subject?" Carolus asked Rumble.

Rumble smiled again.

"If I had, I shouldn't say," he replied.

"I hope there's not going to be any more," announced Mrs Rumble. "One's quite enough to upset us all."

When Carolus left she followed him to the door.

"What do you think I ought to do about those galoshes?" she asked.

"I think you should take them to the police and tell them where you found them."

"Who? Slatt?"

"Yes. He's your local policeman. They may have some bearing on the case."

"You think they were Miss Griggs's, then?"

"I think it's very likely."

"I'll run round with them straight away," said Mrs Rumble. "I shouldn't want anyone to think I'd Take anything."

"Of course not."

She hesitated.

"Nearly new, they are. Just my size. Still if you say it's best I'll run round with them."

"Do you mind if I see them? " Carolus asked.

For one moment Mrs Rumble hesitated, then she said —"No. I don't mind. I'll fetch them in a minute."

Carolus examined a pair of brown galoshes, size eight, nearly new and made by Skilley and Harman.

"Yes, I shall run round with them at once," repeated Mrs Rumble regretfully.

"Good-night. Thank you for my tea."

7

CAROLUS wondered whether he was not treating the case in too leisurely a manner, but reflected as he had often done that criminology must remain nothing to him but a hobby. He had no intention of neglecting the job of teaching which he had set himself because without it he was in danger of becoming a mere rich dilettante. The discipline imposed by school life was, he knew, the one thing which kept him from all the fatuous forms of time-wasting practised by people who had money and no occupation.

So when a case like this came along, however keen his curiosity and however strong his determination to discover the truth, he could only pursue his enquiries when his duties at the Queen's School, Newminster, permitted him to do so. If the police succeeded before him, or made an arrest while he was still asking questions, it would be just too bad. He could do nothing to prevent it.

Besides, as he had always recognized, his method was not a rapid one. He had a gift for making people confide in him but it took time to hear them and it was fatal to attempt to hurry them. Out of those confidences would emerge the truth, a hint here, an odd fact there, and slowly the whole thing would fall into shape. But he had to take his time.

Even so, however conscientiously he might stick to his work at Newminster, he felt that his frequent absences after school hours had not escaped the attention of Mr Gorringer and that sooner or later he would be faced with one of the headmaster's semi-confidential, for-your-own-good orations. It came sooner than Carolus thought. He found himself one morning striding up and down the quadrangle beside Mr Gorringer, whose hands were clasped behind him under the folds of his gown. The headmaster was even more facetious than Carolus had feared.

"A bird has whispered in my ear . . ." he began.

Carolus stared with stupefaction at the huge hairy orifice surrounded with tufted chasms which the head-master had mentioned and wondered what bird would dare approach its sinister network. A vulture, perhaps.

"That our Senior History Master is again immersed in the contemporary. That you, Deene, albeit with a dis-cretion for which I am glad, are once more, as it were, on the trail."

Carolus wondered. Should he quote Kipling? 'The Long Trail—the trail that is always new'. On the whole, no.

"And unless Rumour plays us false, it is the village of Gladhurst which claims so much of your time."

Mr Gorringer was hardest to bear when he was playful.

"That's right," said Carolus.

"An interesting case?" queried Mr Gorringer.

"Quite."

"That, no doubt, accounts for your hasty departures from Newminster," said the headmaster in a rather more serious voice. "Oh, believe me, Deene, I make no stricture. I recognize each man's right to his private interests. I have not openly criticized Hollingbourne's predilection

64

for poultry-keeping on a scale which might almost be termed avicultural though I am relieved to know that as he has accepted the housemastership of Plantagenet he will reduce his stock to domestic dimensions. Even Beardley's commercial interest in antiques has met no more than a meaning frown from me. I am not on this, as on previous occasions, requiring that you should desist from your enquiries for I recognize that in your more recent cases you have shown a greater discretion than of yore. I only ask that in pursuing your hobby you do not involve us all. That your position as Senior History Master here is not a matter to be bandied to and fro by all and sundry and that in no case should the Press be aware of it."

"I'll do my best."

"My wife joins me in her solicitude, though she was unable to resist a witticism when she heard the name of the murdered lady. 'Mr Deene', she said, 'is doubtless out to discover why the sea is boiling hot, and whether Griggs have wings.' I must say, I derived considerable amusement from the *mot*."

"Yes," said Carolus, unable to think of another comment.

"Very well, my dear Deene, I have full confidence in you. I must have a word with the music master. Ah, Tubley . . ."

Even his housekeeper seemed less disturbed by the participation of Carolus in a case so far away than she had been on other occasions.

"Well, I must allow," she said when she brought in his lunch, "that if you will get yourself mixed up in crimes and horrors I wish they was all like this one. I was only saying to Stick, there's scarcely been a word in the newspapers and not a soul calling here at all hours without our knowing if it was a murderer or not. Are you going over there again this afternon, Sir?"

"Yes, Mrs Stick. I have to meet several more of the inhabitants."

"Then you be careful and don't eat or drink anything when you don't know where it's from. You oughtn't to be hanging about after dark, either. If they can do for an old lady they can do for you, make no mistake."

"Thank you, Mrs Stick, I'll be careful. Leave me out some sandwiches in case I'm late."

"There! And I'd got a nice piece of turbot for your dinner and was going to make you a Creep Suzette to follow. I shall wait till half-past eight and if you're not here I shan't cook at all. I won't serve things rechauffay, so it's no good asking me to."

When Carolus reached Gladhurst in a driving rain-storm he decided to postpone once more his meeting with Grazia Vaillant from whom he expected most and call on the churchwarden, Commander Fyfe.

'He is not', Mrs Bobbin had said, 'what you would imagine a retired naval officer to be like'. Carolus tried to imagine what a retired naval officer *would* be like but his effort was unsuccessful. Beefy and boisterous? Ginny and garrulous? Prosy and pompous? Jovial and judicious? He might be anything.

But Mrs Bobbin had been right. Whatever retired naval officers were like they were not like Commander Fyfe.

His house, called The Fairway, was at the end of the village farthest from the church, a stucco and slated affair closely hidden by trees. Relieved to see a porch over the front door Carolus ran from his car to its shelter, then rang the bell.

As he stood there he had an uncomfortable feeling that he was being watched and, noticing a mirror set in the door's panel, he guessed that it was one of those con-structed to allow one behind it to see through while appearing an ordinary mirror from the outside. He at once made a grimace at it and a rude sign with his fingers.

Then a small trap in the main door opened and for the first time he had a glimpse of the narrow bald head,

66

the active dark eyes, the vigorous growth of eyebrow and the thin clean-shaven lips of the churchwarden.

" Oh yes, I know," said Fyfe. " Your name's Deene, isn't it? Wait a minute while I unbolt this door."

' A minute ' turned out to be three and the scraping and grating, the rattling and jangling suggested that Fyfe was the custodian of one of our less escape-prone prisons.

" Come in," said Fyfe conspiratorially and, when Carolus was standing in a dark passage, set to work to bolt, bar, chain and lock behind them.

" Come to my den. We shall be undisturbed there. You don't mind if I lock the door? Sit down, please. Smoke? Listen! What's that? "

" It sounds like the rain," said Carolus.

" It *may* be. It may be. But you never know. Get some queer noises round here. Very queer. It's a queer place altogether. Have to take every precaution."

" So I notice. Against what? "

" Against what? Well, you know what's just happened. Poor woman clubbed. I put nothing past them."

" Past whom? "

" Any of them. I tell you this place is full of strange characters. Have you met a woman known as ' Flo '? "

" I've seen her. I should have thought she was the most harmless of souls."

" She may be. But indiscreet. Loud-mouthed. I was foolish enough to stop and chat with her one afternoon. Merely to ask how she was. I had seen her in church. I assure you I didn't stop for more than two minutes. Yet before I reached home my wife had heard of it. The vicar knew. The whole village. It caused me a great deal of inconvenience. Of course the woman herself didn't mind at all."

" No, Flo doesn't mind," repeated Carolus.

" That's only one of the things." Fyfe turned round suddenly and looked at the window. " Did you see any-thing? " he asked.

67

"Trees," said Carolus.

"I thought I noticed a shadow. As though someone were outside. I may be mistaken. Can't be too careful. What did you want to ask me?"

"About the day of the murder."

Fyfe nearly leapt from his chair.

"That *was* a day," he said. "Extraordinary things happened that day."

"Such as?"

Fyfe leant forward.

"It was on that day," he confided, "that the incident happened which I have described to you. With the woman known as Flo."

"Where?"

"In the very centre of the village. Outside Jevons's Stores. It couldn't have been less secretive. Yet . . ."

"At about what time did you meet her?"

"That I can tell you exactly. Habit of mine. Always make a note of the times of events. You never know, you see. Anything can happen in a place like this. It was 3.48. I need scarcely add p.m."

"So you were in the village street between half-past three and . . . when, would you say?"

"Nearly four."

"Whom did you meet?"

"That's the extraordinary thing. Almost no one."

"Almost?"

"I saw Slipper, our curate, you know. Very good with boys."

"So I understand. Was he on foot?"

"Yes. Hurrying along as he usually is. Wearing a raincoat."

"Alone?"

"That's another strange thing. He was alone. Usually has several of the boys with him."

"You saw no one else?"

"Only the girl who works at Crossways. Naomi Chester."

" Did she see you? "

" I think not. I was in the Post Office. I saw her pass on the other side of the road."

" On foot? "

" Yes. She too was in a hurry."

" Going towards her home? "

" It might be. Yes. One doesn't know of course."

" You reached home at what time? "

" Soon after four. I found the vicar here."

" Mrs Fyfe was at home? "

" Yes. As I have explained, she had already heard this extraordinary story about the woman called Flo."

" Oh yes. Perhaps the vicar himself had told her? "

" No. I understand someone had made a telephone call. Shows you, doesn't it? Small place like this. Full of malice. Old women, you know."

" Yes. You do seem to have a collection of somewhat irascible elderly women. I understand a man called Grey was working for you."

" No. No. Not for me. He is employed by a local firm of builders and decorators. He was painting. The dining-room."

" You found him there when you returned that afternoon? "

" No. Just gone. Quite extraordinary. A phone call had come for him. My wife answered the phone."

" Who wanted him? "

" My wife didn't recognize the voice. That of an elderly woman, she thinks."

" Another elderly woman? "

" So my wife tells me. She did not listen to the conversation. She told Grey he was wanted on the phone and noticed that shortly after he left the house."

" Before his usual time? "

" Yes. Very odd, wasn't it? "

" You didn't by any chance pass the churchyard that afternoon? "

" It was the first thing I did after lunch." Fyfe's voice

69

dropped almost to a whisper. "Rumble was there. At work on Chilling's grave."

"There was surely nothing odd about that, Commander Fyfe? Chilling was to be buried next day."

"But do you know who was helping him? Mugger, of all people."

"Yes. Rumble told me."

"A dangerous character, that."

"Dangerous?"

"Lawless. Violent."

"He has the freedom of your land, I believe."

"What? Oh, rabbits, yes. He helps to keep the rabbits down."

Dusk had fallen as they talked but Commander Fyfe did not switch on the lights. They sat in half darkness. Fyfe's voice was hollow and awed and his eyes restless.

"You didn't notice anyone hanging about outside when you came in?" he asked Carolus.

"No. Why?"

"You can't be too careful. Yes, Rumble and Mugger were digging the grave and Rumble was actually singing as he worked. I could tell you something else."

"Yes?"

"The three old ladies—well, there are only two of them now—have a nephew who lives at Burley."

"I have a note of that, I think."

"But you didn't know he was over here that afternoon, did you? In his car. A grey Vauxhall. Saw him with my own eyes. You see what I mean when I say queer things happen in this place."

"Not quite. What is extraordinary about Dundas Griggs?"

"He is the nephew of the murdered woman," gasped Fyfe.

"I see."

"And he was in Gladhurst on the day of the murder."

"Mm."

70

"Then what about Larkin?" whispered Fyfe.

"What about him?"

"You surely know his connection?"

"I know that there is a story that more than forty years ago there was some incident connecting him with Millicent Griggs."

"There you are! I tell you . . ."

"Did you go out again that day, Commander Fyfe?"

"I? My wife is an invalid, as you may have heard. I never go out at night and leave her alone in the house. Certainly not. Anything might happen. Anything. But on that evening I was fortunate. My gardener and his wife who live nearby had asked leave to view the television. I took advantage of that for a brief spell."

"What time would that have been?"

"Oh, six-thirty to eight, perhaps."

"Did you remain downstairs long after that?"

"Oh, an hour or two, I daresay. With my stamps, you know. I am a philatelist."

"You heard nothing more of the outside world, as it were, that evening?"

"At one point I thought I heard someone tapping on that window pane. But I found it was the branch of a tree."

"Very disappointing for you. Nothing more?"

"Motor-cycles," said Commander Fyfe.

"That was not unusual though?"

"In winter? On this road? Most."

Carolus rose.

"I shall have to open the door for you. I'll tell you if anything else very strange occurs."

"Thank you," said Carolus. "I wonder what you could tell me about the dead woman? Her character, I mean?"

It had occurred to Carolus that unreliable and sensational as Fyfe might be on facts, on character he would be more dependable.

"Strange, very strange," he said, shaking his head. "I

cannot pretend that she was popular—very much the contrary. She was a woman of insatiable curiosity. Of a most unsavoury kind, I fear. I was once rash enough to leave her alone in conversation with my wife. My dear fellow, the *questions* she asked. I could scarcely believe it afterwards. Hair-raising."

"She doesn't sound very pleasant."

"Pleasant? She was . . . but the woman is dead so let's say no more. Now I'll let you out if you like."

The unbolting began again.

"Have to take precautions," explained Fyfe.

It was still raining as Carolus drove away.

8

Now there was nothing for it. He must call on Grazia Vaillant.

He found the Old Vicarage a well-kept house, vaguely Georgian in architecture, with additions probably made by the fathers of large families in the last century. But as soon as he drew near he saw that no opportunity had been missed for antique embellishment. Wrought iron gates had been put in, large urns evidently from Crowthers' topped the gateposts, beside the front door was a huge ship's bell and over it a ship's lamp. A wrought iron bracket which had once had a sign swinging from it had been fixed to the wall with another lamp suspended from it. An antique sundial was on the lawn and an ancient dovecote was visible.

Mrs Rumble opened the door. She was evidently a woman who having taken the unprecedented step of according someone her friendship did not turn back, for she made a grimace at Carolus which was intended to suggest a smile.

" I was just off," she confided. " But she's in, all right. Having her tea. Wait here a minute and I'll tell her."

Carolus stood among coffin-stools and oak chests, corner cupboards and brass chestnut-roasters, cricket-tables and warming-pans, arranged not as they had been in the place in which they should have stayed, some expensive Old Curiosity Shop in Rye or Tunbridge Wells, but as though they were the natural furniture of the house.

Presently Mrs Rumble reappeared and ushered him to a large drawing-room. Grazia Vaillant came forward to greet him with extended hand and they met under an enormous glass chandelier which tinkled no more than Grazia herself with her pendants and bits and pieces. She wore something which William Morris might have designed for the châtelaine of an old English castle. Her hair was henna-red and her eyes searching and hungry.

Carolus had time to observe the room about him, a nightmare of old samplers, stump-work pictures, Dresden figures, half a dozen clocks such as collectors value, an antique hour-glass, a couple of spinning-wheels, a collection of tea-caddies, stools with woolwork covers and a spinet. But over the fireplace was a magnificent landscape which looked as though it had entered by mistake. Almost certainly a Constable, Carolus thought.

" How do you *Doo*? " asked Grazia, forgetting to release Carolus's hand. " Come to the fire and have some tea. Such a wretched day. I hear you're investigating our murder."

" Yes, in a way."

" Such a dreadful, dreadful business."

" I'm glad to see you're not scared by it, Miss Vaillant. You remain alone here at night? "

" But of course. I have my *ange gardien*."

" Useful. Any watchdog? "

" Oh yes. Peter and Paul my two boxers. Oh, *I*'m all right, I assure you. Besides, lightning doesn't strike in the same place twice. Why should we expect anything more

73

in Gladhurst? They have the jewellery and money, poor old Millicent Griggs is dead. Aren't we entitled to peace now? "

"'They'. Who do you mean by 'they'? "

"The robbers. The murderers."

"I see. You had not been friendly with Miss Griggs, I believe? "

"We are all Christians, Mr Deene, but I did have to remind myself of it rather often with Millicent Griggs. She *was* so painfully protty. . . ."

"I'm sorry. I don't know that word."

"Protestant."

"But—forgive my ignorance—I thought that was your religion. Church of England, I mean."

"No. No, Mr Deene," smiled Grazia kindly. "You've got it all wrong. We're Car-tholics."

"But? "

"Not Romans, of course. Just Car-tholics. The Church of England is part of the Car-tholic Church."

"What are the other parts? "

"The Orthodox Russian. The Greek. The Roman. All one."

"I see. But Miss Griggs wasn't included? "

"You are naughty," said Grazia Vaillant. "She was what is called evangelical, though I can't think why they use that lovely word. She opposed every effort we made to beautify our church, to make it more in keeping with its heritage. We had struggle after struggle. . . ."

"Who did? How did the vicar vote? "

"Poor Father Waddell! He's rather a waverer, you know. I remember when I gave him a beautiful set of Stations of the Cross by a Spanish artist, he hesitated. He was wondering what Millicent Griggs would say. You see, to her, Mr Deene, I was the Scarlet Woman, I was Popery personified. She really believed I kept Jesuit priests in hiding-holes and was planning another Gunpowder Plot. She hated me and all I stood for with the hatred of a Puritan for a Cavalier."

74

" And you? "

" God gave me a sense of humour," claimed Grazia, waving a heavily bangled arm. " I was able to see the funny side of poor old Millicent especially when I once nipped over to the church and gave it a good censing with the best incense just before their dreary old Eleven O'Clock Service which Father Waddell *will* keep on to please them. Millicent really thought Father Waddell had been using incense at Sung Mass—she never comes to that. She rose in her pew and said in a ringing voice, ' Incense is an abomination to me! Isaiah 1, XIII, 1.' Then she marched out of the church. Father Waddell was very cross with me. He had to go and explain that I had done it as a joke. ' Such jokes ', said Millicent, ' will call down fire and brimstone from heaven utterly to consume the wicked '. You see the sort of thing? Yes, she hated me, all right, but I could only find her funny and stuffy and protty, poor old thing."

" I hear there was a reconciliation."

" If you call it that," said Grazia Vaillant, pouring another cup of tea for Carolus. "You see I was most anxious to have a Lady Chapel. When I tackled Father Waddell he took refuge in a kind of diplomacy which I can't say I admired. ' If you can get Millicent Griggs to agree, yes,' he said. ' If you can't talk her round I shall have to say no.' So I went to work and asked her here to tea. She was very much on her guard at first but I put it in the most modest way. A matter of convenience, I said, to save light when there are only a few people. ' You already have the Lord's Table ', she said. ' I know, but we want two Lord's Tables ', I said. ' If you don't object to one why should you object to two? ' Rather clever of me, I thought, and very soon I saw she was coming round. She asked how many candlesticks would be on it, and I said only two. She agreed to give me her answer two days later and came round again. This time she asked whether I would subscribe to one of her pet charities—to convert the Jews or something. When I agreed she said she would not stand in the way of what she called the second Lord's Table. She little knew that I'd bought a great big statue of Our Lady of Lourdes all ready for it."

"So the vicar now agreed?"

"Well, it was only two days before she was murdered, poor old thing, and of course we've all been rather upset since then."

"Naturally."

"I was often very angry with her. She was infuriating, sometimes. She called everything we did to restore the church to its old state an *innovation*. You could not make her see that Protestantism itself was an innovation and our religion the old one. Whenever I did some perfectly *natural* thing like cross myself or kneel for a part of the Creed she looked at me as though she would like to strangle me. She wasn't quite sane, you know."

"I certainly didn't know. Are you serious?"

"Quite. I won't say she was certifiable, though the sister Flora really is. But unbalanced. You couldn't have such ferocity in a normal mind. She once threatened me with her umbrella because someone told her my position with regard to Transubstantiation. She blamed me for everything. I was 'plotting and scheming' to undermine what she called the 'grand old English church service'. That sort of thing. It was an obsession with her. She spoke of me as 'that Popish Vaillant woman'. There was a time when I really thought she would do me some physical injury. Can you call that sane?"

"Your disagreement does seem to have gone to some lengths. It is surprising that you should have been reconciled."

"We weren't, really. Things were just patched up. She never ceased to hate me. She admitted that she would like to see me dead. She believed, sincerely believed, that an avenging fire would strike me from heaven."

"No!"

"Truthfully. She told her sister Flora that, on the day before she died. 'Not long', she said. Then changing the sex in the words, she quoted Isaiah again. 'Woe unto the wicked! it shall be ill with her: for the doing of her hands shall be done to her.' Then she went on, quoting correctly, ' As for my people, children are their oppressors and women rule over them.' "

" How do you know this? "

" Rumble heard it and told his wife. She told me."

" It's very interesting."

" It did not worry me. I know that kind of Calvinism."

" Are there many people in the parish who felt as you did about—er, ritual and so on? "

" You really do put things in an odd way. If by 'ritual and so on' you mean the Car-tholic religion, oh yes, there are a number of good folk who want to see dear Father Waddell take a firm line. The Miller-Wrights, for instance, are sound enough on vestments though they buck at a Sanctus bell. The Wilmingtons go all the way, bless them, though Moira Wilmington confided in me once that she always gets stuck on Eternal Damnation. The Skiptons we are educating nicely—they've got as far as Sung Eucharist and I *think* were coming round to auricular confession."

" But the working people? "

" My old Mrs Rumble is a great comfort. She doesn't know what it's all about but she wants things brightened up, she says. Then have you heard of a woman known as Flo? "

" Have I *not!* "

" A teeny bit of a Mary Magdalene, I gather. Not very particular in her morals. But she has the right idea. She used to go to St Christopher's Hoxton in the great days of Father Wemyss-Buchan. She's been well taught."

" You mean she goes to church? "

" Well, not very often. I *did* persuade her to attend our Midnight Mass last Christmas. (There was endless trouble with the Griggses about holding that and Father Waddell got over it by promising them a Watch Night Service on

New Year's Eve.) But I can't pretend poor Flo is a regular communicant. I don't think she's a really bad woman. Just hopelessly compliant. I blame the men of the village."

"She seems an amiable soul."

"There were one or two others with the right ideas. And several more who would have been all right if the Griggses had left them alone."

"Tell me, what about the other clergyman? Mr Slipper?"

"Father Slipper? Oh, he was all right. Good little chap. Did as he was told. Left all decisions to Father Waddell."

"Was he—er, High Church or Low? If those are the correct terms."

"Your education has been neglected, Mr Deene. We don't speak of High Church. That goes back to Victorian days. As I have told you, we are Car-tholics."

"Is that what is meant when people speak of Anglo-Catholic?"

"I suppose so but 1 don't like the term."

"And Mr Slipper?"

"All right on most things. All the Sacraments except Extreme Unction. Celibacy of the Clergy, the Assumption, the Immaculate Conception, all sound. A bit shaky on Reservation and Benediction. But his heart's in the right place."

"He organizes things for the youth of the parish?"

"Wonderful with boys. Open air, you know. Healthy. Scouting and cycling. Organizes camps in the summer. He has persuaded old Sir Marriott Gibson to let them use the swimming pool in his grounds."

"And in the winter?"

"Oh, he has his Club and Scout headquarters. Always arranging something. A play or physical culture. Weight-lifting for the older ones. I hear they're entering a team for some competition. They all walk about as though they couldn't forget their shoulders. Waygooze, our organist, gets quite fed up with them flexing their muscles when they ought to be learning the *Kyrie Eleison*. But there's no doubt Father Slipper does a lot of good."

" Did Miss Griggs recognize that? "

" I think so. She gave him a subscription whenever he asked for it. It was she who bought new bell tents for them last summer. I gather she has left money in her will both to Father Slipper and his pet causes."

Grazia was gathering together the New Hall tea-service and putting it on the old Sheffield plate tray, with a jolly tinkle of beads and bangles.

" Of course from *my* point of view it's all very well, this youth organization, but I can't help feeling that a priest should be a priest and not a physical training instructor or expert on cooking over a fire in the open. I should like to see more catechism and less camp for the boys. But that's no doubt my old-fashioned point of view. I don't say Father Slipper doesn't get many of them to church but if they have to be induced to sing together in the choir by being allowed to sleep in tents, it doesn't seem to *me* to be putting first things first."

" I suppose not."

" There's a great deal of good in it, no doubt. But you know in a small place like this where there is sufficient labour, I'm *not* convinced that their bob-a-job scheme is so good. The boys hang round the cottages willing to lend a hand but most of them have very little to offer. It seems to me that Father Slipper is groping after something but never seems to find what he wants. However you don't need to hear my views. It's facts you're after. What can I tell you? "

" Mr Waddell tells me that he called to see you on the evening Miss Griggs died and that you were out."

" The silly man! I was nothing of the sort! I may have been having a little snooze—I often do about that time. In fact now I come to think of it I remember waking up and finding I hadn't yet put on the lights and the tea things were still out."

79

"What time was that?"

"It must have been nearly seven. Shocking, wasn't it? Sloth, one of the Seven Deadly Sins. If Father Waddell had only pulled at my old ship's bell instead of just pressing the electric one he would have awakened me."

"Did you go out at all that day?"

"To early Mass, yes. Father Slipper said it that morning. We've managed to persuade Father Waddell to have a daily Mass though he has to call it Communion. The Griggs contingent would have a fit if he didn't. . . ."

"But later in the day?"

"Let's see. I don't think I did. It was cold, I remember."

"Not in the afternoon or evening, anyhow?"

"I'm *sure* I didn't. I always do the flowers on Tuesdays and Saturdays at the church. No. I stayed in that day. Like a dormouse."

"You heard or saw nothing which might be helpful?"

"Nothing, I'm afraid. My good Mrs Rumble told me her husband was digging a grave for Chilling, I remember."

"You didn't enter the church?"

"No, Mr Deene."

"I don't think there's anything else I need ask you, Miss Vaillant. Unless you care to throw any light on one of the small mysteries—that of your reconciliation with Millicent Griggs. It does puzzle me that after years of antagonism she should have come here twice in a week."

"It puzzled me," said Grazia Vaillant immediately. "But I've told you all about it."

"I haven't yet met Miss Flora Griggs. Do you think she shared in her sister's kindlier feelings?"

"I'm not sure that Millicent's feelings were kindlier. If they were, Flora certainly did not share in them. She has a sort of Old Testament hatred for poor me."

Carolus's eyes went back to that landscape—the only beautiful thing in the room.

80

"Ah—you're looking at my Constable," said Grazia. "Fine, isn't it?" She threw out her hand. "Good-bye!" she said.

Carolus said good-bye with some relief and left Grazia Vaillant among her antiques.

It was still raining and a dark night but the ship's light over the door had been switched on and he could go quickly down the crazy pavement path to his car.

He started the engine, but when he switched on the lights he saw someone hurrying towards him, gesticulating to indicate that he should wait.

There came into his head absurd things like Mrs Stick's warning—'you oughtn't to be hanging about after dark, either. If they can do for an old lady they can do for you'. And Commander Fyfe's questions about people 'hanging about'.

When he recognized the approaching figure he remembered also Fyfe's description of him as 'a dangerous character, lawless, violent'. For the man who had stopped him was Mugger.

9

Mugger had a thin insinuating voice. It might have been that in which Brer Fox addressed Brer Rabbit. He brought his long solemn face, with its ginger hair visible under his cap, to the window of Carolus's car, and Carolus opened this by a few inches. The rain was pelting down on him but seemed to have no effect as though his very skin were rainproof.

"I want to speak to you," he said.

"You'd better get into the car," Carolus told him and the long thin man twined in, scarcely opening the door. There was a silence.

81

"It was Rumble told me about you," said Mugger at last, the tone of his voice not changing. "He said it would be all right if I told you."

"What's that?"

"Something," said Mugger promptly and flatly.

Carolus with his usual patience, waited.

"You're not a copper, are you?" said Mugger.

"No."

"You wouldn't say anything?"

Carolus was greatly tempted to give a promise. But he had to come out with the old prim line which sounded so odd, spoken here in half-darkness in the rain-washed car.

"It depends on what you tell me. I'll only promise to respect your confidence as far as I honestly can. You see, you might tell me something which would have a direct bearing on the recent murder case. What could I do then?"

"I want to show you something."

"Even then, how do I know that it won't be my duty to report it?"

"I don't know what to do," said Mugger. "And I'm not a man not to know what to do. I saw you talking to Slatt the other night. Did he say anything about me?"

"No."

"I give *him* a hard time. See, I don't say I'm an angel."

"No."

"Nor yet a psalm-singing hypocrite. I like a bit of fun," said Mugger lugubriously.

"What sort of fun?" asked Carolus, falling headlong into the trap.

"Well, not too old. Nor yet so young it'll get you into trouble. About twenty-five or thirty with a nice big chassis who don't open her mouth too wide."

"That wasn't exactly what I asked. However, do you find your bit of fun in Gladhurst?"

Mugger looked gloomier.

"Of course I do. It's everywhere, if you know how to look for it. There's one working out at Ryley's farm. . . ."

"Don't let's go into details."

"Well, you asked me. I mean, where should we be without it? You can't have all work and no play, can you? I remember one lived in Church Cottages. You've never seen anyone like it. It was as though she was on fire. . . ."

"You had something to tell me, I believe?"

"I was telling you about this one, lived in Church Cottages. I had to tell her in the end she'd get me into trouble if my old woman got to hear of anything. Then there was a German one came to work for some people here. Oh dear, oh dear. I shall never forget it. She was tall as I was, very near, but big-made with it. There *was* a lot of her. I used to say to her, ' there *is* a lot of you ', I used to say, but of course she never understood a word of English. Then when I was rabbiting one night. . . ."

"Look, Mugger, I'm sure your reminiscences are very interesting. You ought to write a book some day. But I'm trying to find out about Miss Griggs, not about your various adventures. If you've got anything to tell me, let's have it. If not I'll drop you off where you like."

"Well, I have got something to tell you but I don't know how you'll take it."

"I'm afraid I can't give you any assurance on that. I certainly shan't talk for the sake of talking."

"I don't know what to say. Suppose I was to hint to you, no more than a hint, mind, that I might know where a bit of jewellery was to be seen?"

"You mean? Oh, I see. Good heavens, man, you can't keep that. You'll find yourself charged with murder if you're found in possession of it."

"That's what I'm afraid of. But I'm not in possession of it. I've left it where I found it."

"What about the money?"

"There was no money," said Mugger and for the first

time a touch of animation was in his voice. "No money, there wasn't. Not a sausage. Jools. No money."

"Have you done any work since helping Rumble to dig Chilling's grave? "

"Work? No. To tell the truth I haven't had time. There's one come to live with her auntie just near the station. Just right, she is. You know, not too thin and not a big sack of potatoes either. Only thing is she won't come out of doors. Says it's too cold. So I have to wait till her auntie's out. . . ."

Mugger's long face expressed nothing but gloom.

"You haven't worked for a couple of weeks yet you don't seem short of money."

"Oh well. Got to have a bit of luck sometime. But those jools are just as I found them. Something told me not to touch them. But I want a bit out of them, mind. I'm entitled to that, for finding them."

"That will be up to the family."

"Oh. But I haven't said where they are yet, have I? If I'm not going to get anything out of it they can go on searching. Then they'll probably never know who did for the old girl."

"Don't you think you're being rather rash? "

"Always have been," said Mugger sadly. "It's a miracle my old woman's never tumbled anything. There was one lived two doors from us, getting on a bit, she was, but still what you might call all right. I used to see her. . . ."

"Yes, yes. I'm sure you've been most successful. But being found out by your wife is rather different from a charge by the police."

"I don't worry about police. Never have. Take Slatt, for instance. He's been after me for years."

"But, Mugger, this is what is called a murder case."

"Still, I didn't do it, did I? "

"I don't know. But the police will regard your keeping the stolen jewellery hidden as at least half a case against you."

"I can prove I had nothing to do with it. Soon as I'd
84

finished with Rumble that afternoon I went home to tea. My old woman can vouch for that. Then, naming no names, I had to meet someone just about the time when Slatt seems to think old Miss Griggs was done for. Just after dark, that was."

"I daresay you have an alibi of sorts. But not reporting your find amounts to being an accessory after the fact, or something of the sort."

"So you think I ought to just hand it over and perhaps never get a thank you?"

"I'm afraid so. After all there *was* the money, wasn't there?"

"What money? I told you there was no money."

"I know you did."

"Calling me a liar, are you?"

"Of course I am. Now, look, Mugger, don't be silly. You've had your reward for finding it and as long as the bank hasn't got the numbers of the notes. . . ."

"Do you think they might have?"

"Not if they were in one-pound notes. Fivers and above they probably will have taken."

Mugger's lugubrious voice seemed to rise to a more cheerful pitch.

"Anyhow, there wasn't any money. Want to see the jools? Then you'll know what's best to be done. Though I'm not a man to ask anyone that, generally. I'm a quiet man and know how to go about my business my own way."

"Where are they?" asked Carolus.

There was a long sigh from the lugubrious Mugger.

"I suppose I shall have to tell you and chance it," he said.

He sat there immobile and melancholy. In the light of the dashboard Carolus could see the lantern jaws and the red hair, the expression of set inviolable solemnity.

"Do *you* want a bit of fun?" asked Mugger, his voice unchanged. "Because I know where one's just come to live. . . ."

85

"Are you going to take me to where this jewellery is hidden or not? " asked Carolus in exasperation.

"All right, all right," moaned Mugger. "I was only asking you if you wanted a bit of fun. No need to have it if you don't want it. Only you won't often see one like this. . . ."

Carolus made to start the car.

"You don't need no car," said Mugger. "Leave it here and come with me."

Carolus turned up the collar of his overcoat and prepared to follow. The rain persisted although a light wind had arisen.

"Got a torch? " asked Mugger.

Carolus pulled one from the pocket of the car.

Mugger led the way across the open space in front of the church and it was obvious that he was making for the lych-gate. In the shelter of this they waited for a moment.

"This is a handy place," confided Mugger, "if you've got one with you on a wet night. No one's going to disturb you here. They keep away from churchyards after dark. I remember . . ."

"Come along," said Carolus.

Mugger led the way by a path which passed the West door and went round by the South side of the church. They were rather more sheltered here. Carolus could just make out the shapes of gravestones as his eyes became accustomed to the darkness. Finally Mugger opened a door rather below ground level and they entered what was evidently the furnace-room mentioned by Rumble as the place where his tools were kept. It was cold enough tonight to be an ice-store. Carolus threw the light of his torch in every direction.

"See, this is where Rumble keeps his spades for when he has a grave to dig. But he only just comes in and out again except when he gets the furnace going. He never goes up those steps."

Carolus saw that against the wall was an iron ladder,

leading, evidently, to some kind of loft. He followed Mugger up these and found himself under a sloping roof too low to allow him to stand upright.

"I've used this for years," said Mugger. "Keep my rabbiting wires and gun and cartridges here besides one or two other things I use when I go out at night. I don't suppose you'd know how to collect half a dozen pheasants in an evening, would you? Besides, I need somewhere to put anything I find. Old Slatt would have given his right hand to know of this which is one reason I don't like bringing the coppers here. Of course I've moved all my stuff now but the new place isn't nearly so good. Now look at this."

Near the top of the steps was an old toolbox which Mugger opened and Carolus at once saw what Mugger described as 'the jools'. There was a collection such as a rich and ostentatious elderly woman might have worn in the daytime, several bracelets, four rings, a large diamond brooch and a necklet.

"When did you find these?"

"On the night after the murder."

"And the money?"

Mugger answered as though Carolus had been tactless.

"I've told you there was no money," he said. "Anything I found was all together in this box. Whoever it was must have known Rumble kept his spade here and come to get it to throw in enough soil to cover her. When he brought the spade back he was wondering where to get rid of the jools till things had blown over a bit and seen those steps. I don't suppose it took him a minute to nip up and pop them in here."

"You haven't touched these?" asked Carolus.

"I know enough for that," said Mugger. "If I'd been going to take them I'd have taken them. If not there was no call to leave my fingerprints all over them."

"Very wise."

"I suppose there's a decent bit of money in that lot, isn't there?" asked Mugger.

"I imagine so. I'm not an expert. Now I have to drive back through Burley. Would you like me to drop you off at the police station there?"

"Whatever for?"

"You're going to report this, aren't you?"

"I suppose I've got to if you say so. Only I'm not going over to Burley for that. Slatt'll do for me."

So Mugger once again settled into Carolus's car and they drove to the cottage distinguished from the rest by a sign outside bearing the words COUNTY POLICE. The door was opened by a thin woman, presumably the policeman's wife.

"I suppose you'd better come in as it's raining," she said.

Slatt entered the room where they waited, his jaws still working.

"I was just having my tea," he announced unnecessarily.

An extraordinary expression, half ghoulish, half mischievous, came over Mugger's face and Carolus supposed that he was smiling.

"What do you want, Mugger?" asked Slatt sternly. "And you're the man asking me questions the other night. What is it you both want?"

Mugger was not to be hurried.

"Got one for you this time, Slatt," he said.

"Have you something to report?" asked the policeman grandly.

"Got right ahead of you this time, Slatt. Left you a long way behind."

Carolus could not resist quoting *Hudibras.*

"*Quoth Hudibras, Friend Ralph, thou hast
Outrun the constable at last.*"

Slatt turned on him furiously.

"Police officer!" he shouted.

"I beg your pardon," said Carolus.

88

*"Quoth Hudibras, Friend Ralph, thou hast
Outrun the Police Officer at last."*

"What's this all about?"
"How would you like to know where Miss Griggs's
jools are?" asked Mugger.
"Are you trying to be funny?"
"Yes," admitted Mugger. "But I know where the jools
are, all the same."
"Then it's your duty to report it to me."
"What do you think I've come here for on a pouring
night like this when I might be in the Black Horse? Of
course I'm going to report it. Get your notebook out and
I'll tell you."
Like a man mesmerized, Slatt obeyed.
"I hope this isn't one of your larks," he said.
"This gentleman will tell you. He's just seen them. It
was him told me to come to you. Otherwise I might have
kept the information to myself."
Slatt had his notebook open.
"When did you make this discovery?" he asked.
"This afternoon. About three o'clock."
Slatt's pencil worked.
"Where?"
"I'm going to take you there in a minute. That's better
than saying."
Slatt nodded and wrote.
"What was there so far as you remember?"
Mugger gave details which Slatt noted.
"Miss Griggs had a sum of money on her," said Slatt.
"There was no money there. Jools, no money."
Slatt said nothing.
"You'll both have to wait a minute while I get on the
telephone to the Detective Inspector in charge of this
case."
He left them together and returned with a smile.
"The D.I. is coming over at once. He'll want you to
take him to the place you found this, Mugger."

" I don't mind," said Mugger. " Even if I have to miss one who's waiting for me in the bus stop shelter. Nothing special, as you might say, but not one of your little bony ones. Something you can get hold of . . ."

" Now Mugger," warned Slatt.

" Well, I'm doing you a favour, aren't I? "

" So you may be but there's no need for Talk. I've got a position to keep up."

" You remember Dogberry? " said Carolus. " Dogberry in *Much Ado About Nothing*. When Seacoal had just been promoted. ' *You are thought here to be the most senseless and fit man to be constable of the Watch* '."

" How many times have I got to tell you? Police Officer, it is."

" Of course. Of course. ' *You are thought here to be the most senseless and fit man to be Police Officer of the Watch* '."

10

At least, thought Carolus, it would give him a chance to meet the CID man in charge of the case, usually a somewhat difficult matter. It was not that professional policemen resented amateurs—they simply did not recognize their existence unless the amateur, by some tactless piece of intrusion, forced them to warn him off matters which did not concern him.

In three of his cases Carolus had been lucky, for his friend John Moore had been in charge of investigations. In one case he had been forced almost to blackmail an obstinate Detective Sergeant into discovering the truth.

In two other cases the police had been sceptical but not obstructive. Now he had a feeling that he would be up against open hostility. Where the police were most baffled they were apt to be irritated by the curiosity of outsiders. An incident like this, a report to them of the whereabouts of Millicent Griggs's jewellery, so far from earning their gratitude for the assistance rendered, would make them peevish and suspicious.

Carolus was not wrong. The Detective Inspector was a small forceful stocky man who sought to take charge of the situation at once. He eyed Carolus and Mugger impatiently.

"Now which of you came on this jewellery?" he asked.

Carolus lit a cigarette and Mugger looked owlish.

"Come along, come along," said Detective Inspector Champer. "We haven't got all night. Which was it?"

Slatt tried to intervene.

"It was Mugger who . . ." he began.

"I'm not asking you," snapped Champer. "Which is Mugger of you two?"

Mugger, without changing his expression, began to speak.

"I don't know whether you've got indigestion," he said sadly. "If so you'd better wait till you're in a proper state to talk to people. I'm going home."

Champer turned to Slatt.

"I thought you said one of these men wanted to show us where he is supposed to have found these jewels?"

"So he did. He told me he'd take me. Mugger it was," said Slatt anxiously.

"Is your name Mugger?" said the Detective Inspector in a more gentle tone.

"Yes," said Mugger and was silent.

"Did you find the jewels?"

"Yes."

Champer turned to Carolus.

"What have you got to do with it?"

Carolus ignored this but again Slatt broke in, this time more successfully.

"It was this gentleman persuaded Mugger to give his information," he explained.

Champer stared at Carolus with open hostility.

"Your name Deene?" he said, and Carolus nodded. "I was told you were hanging round making a nuisance of yourself here. Let me warn you at once, Mr Deene, that I don't like outsiders nosing into any case I'm investigating and what's more I won't have it. You make one move which can be considered obstructing the police and I'll have you in Court at once. You may have found some police officers who have put up with your inquisitiveness —I'm not one of them."

"I've told him," put in Slatt.

"Leave this to me, will you, Slatt? I hope we understand one another, Mr Deene?"

Carolus looked at the little man steadily.

"Did you know that Dundas Griggs, the old lady's nephew, was in Gladhurst on the afternoon of her death?" he asked.

"He . . . What? Don't try to give *me* information. You may have found other senior police officers who thought your statements of some consequence. You won't find that with me. It's scarcely likely that you could have gathered facts we're unaware of. Or do you think you know who killed Millicent Griggs?"

"No. But I think I know *how* she was killed which in this case is all-important. Have a cigarette?"

"What's this about the nephew?" asked Champer suddenly and sulkily.

"Oh nothing. He lives in Burley. Inherits from Millicent Griggs. Was over here in a car on the afternoon of the murder. That's all I know."

Champer grunted.

"Trying, isn't it?" said Carolus. "All this vagueness.

92

I could almost wish another murder would come along and give a lead to the first."

Champer visibly started.

"Another murder?" he said. "What makes you think there's going to be another murder?"

"Oh, not necessarily," said Carolus. "I only thought it might make things coalesce."

"I should have thought that if ever there was a case in which *not* to expect a second murder it was this one. It's a brutal crime with an obvious motive. It's done and I can't see it being repeated."

"You evidently take the view that Millicent Griggs was killed for the sake of immediate robbery?"

"Don't *you*, for heaven's sake?"

"No. I don't. And certainly not in as simple a form as that."

Champer stood up.

"I've no business to be discussing this case with you, Mr Deene. It's against all my principles."

Carolus rose too.

"I'll leave you," he said. "You go and see Mugger's ' jools '. It's quite time I had a drink."

Sturdy little Champer had evidently had enough of this too.

"Good-night, Mr Deene," he said without a smile.

"Good-night, Inspector," returned Carolus, then added infuriatingly—" Odd about those galoshes, wasn't it?"

Champer flushed with irritation.

"What galoshes?" he almost shouted.

"Didn't Mrs Rumble report them after all? Or perhaps your man here didn't think it worth mentioning? I was interested anyway."

Champer's face promised nothing very pleasant for Slatt as Carolus finally escaped into the still persistent rain.

He made straight for the Black Horse and found he was the only customer. George Larkin served him with the large Scotch he ordered and silence fell on the public bar.

For once Carolus was hopelessly at a loss. It was not only the natural surliness of the innkeeper which made him unapproachable—there was something else, a reserve, a hostility, or was it no more than blind stupidity which enshrouded him? If Carolus had been a policeman enquiring he would doubtless have been given some sort of explanation for Larkin's visit to the church or the churchyard on the fatal afternoon, but as a private customer at the pub how could he even bring up the subject?

Suddenly George Larkin spoke.

" S'that right you're trying to find out about the murder? " he asked.

Carolus kept his head and nodded moodily.

" Think you will? "

" I don't know. It's hard going."

George Larkin relapsed into silence. Carolus drank his whisky. No one entered and a minute passed.

" I suppose someone's told you I went up to the church-yard that afternoon? "

Carolus nodded.

" Can't mind their own business in this place. Never have been able to."

" Most small places are like that."

" But not as bad as this one."

Carolus felt as though he was in a fairy story and if he asked a question he would break the spell.

" Yes, I went up there. With my son. 'Bout half-past three it must have been."

" I'll have another Scotch," said Carolus.

George Larkin poured it.

" Wife's grave," he said unexpectedly. " Generally go up there about once a month to see it's decently kept."

" I understand."

" My wife died eight years ago," continued George Larkin; then added the ugly word: " Cancer."

94

Carolus could only nod sympathetically.

"She suffered a lot. She's buried not far from where Chilling's been laid."

"You noticed the open grave then? "

"Yes. Rumble had just finished it."

"You didn't see anyone about except Rumble and Mugger? "

"No. We didn't. We weren't there five minutes."

"Came straight back? "

"Yes. It's a funny thing we happened to go on that afternoon. But there you are."

"Have a drink? " suggested Carolus.

"Thanks. I'll have a bitter. I suppose someone will try and make mischief about us being up there at the time."

At last the door opened and in a moment the public bar was cheered by the bouncing, laughing, talkative personality of the 'woman known as Flo'.

"Well," she said. "You do look a gloomy pair to be sure, standing here with no one in. I'll have a Milk Stout, Mr Larkin. I hear the police have found the jewellery taken from Miss Griggs."

George Larkin stared at her in a stupefied manner.

"Where? " he asked.

"I don't know where but they've found it. Just shows doesn't it? You *do* look a solemn pair and no mistake. You make me feel I want to do Knees Up Mother Brown to wake you up. What a life! Never stops raining, does it? I got soaked coming up Church Lane." She turned to Carolus. "I've seen you before, haven't I? I thought so. Once seen never forgotten. You're not always such a dismal jimmy, are you? I can see I shall have to start cheering you up. They call me a ray of sunshine but you wouldn't say so if you could see me the morning after! Thank you, I don't mind if I do have another. Do you know the story about the man who went to the doctor. . . ."

"Now, Flo," warned George Larkin.

"It's all right. It's not *that* one. I wouldn't tell that one to a stranger. Well, not quite a stranger but you know

95

what I mean. Cheerio! Is that your car outside? You can give me a ride in that one of these days only don't do like old Mr Murdoch did that time and take me right out somewhere then say: 'If you don't, you'll walk back!' Dirty trick, wasn't it? But I didn't mind. He wasn't a bad old fellow. I've known worse anyway. Here, did I ever tell you about that farmer over at Breadley? Proper devil, he was. I began to wonder if I should get out of there alive. Like Bluebeard, really. I thought my last hour had come. But in the end it was nothing. All talk. You do get them, don't you?"

"You ask for it," said George Larkin darkly.

"Oh, I didn't mind. As long as I don't get banged on the head like poor old Miss Griggs. Wicked thing, that was. I never liked her, the old hypocrite, but I don't want to see anyone banged on the head for no fault of their own. I must have missed her by minutes, too. I was in Church Lane that afternoon just after dark. Never mind who with. I was on my way home."

"That's not your way home."

"You know what I mean," said Flo. "I wasn't there above a quarter of an hour. But I never heard anything. Or saw anything. Well, I wasn't thinking of anything like that. It was a nice dark night, not raining like it is now. Oh well, she's Gone, so it's no use our moaning about it. Let's have another Milk Stout and give the gentleman a whisky. A little of what you fancy does you good. I don't believe you're such a Sunday School as you look, if the truth were known. I've seen that quiet kind before. I wouldn't trust *you* far away from home. Not that I've ever been one to push myself. But You Can Tell, can't you? Oh well, anything for a laugh."

"You should really form an understanding with Mugger. He tells me, somewhat graphically, that he 'likes a bit of fun'."

"Fred Mugger? An understanding? Me and old Fred Mugger have been friends for years. You don't want to get taken in by that gloomy face of his. He's a proper Jack-in-

96

the-Box when he gets going. As a matter of fact it was Fred Mugger I was meeting that evening I told you about in Church Lane. What's wrong with that? Even if we did know one another at school. Nice sort of monkey he was then, too. There used to be a shed at the back where they kept wood and that and young Fred, he can't have been more than fourteen years old at the time, got hold of me in there and before I knew where I was, there you were. Yes, it was him I was meeting that night in Church Lane and I remember how angry he was when someone switched his motor-bike headlight on us from the top of the lane when we least expected it. I laughed, of course, but you should have seen his face! "

"I thought you saw no one and heard nothing that night? "

"Nor we didn't because as soon as this motor-bike rider had thrown his lights down the lane and seen us, I suppose, he was Off as fast as he could go. Never came into the lane at all so that to this day I never knew who it was. I didn't mind but it quite upset Fred. You might not think it but he's very shy. Not in what he says but over anything like that. I said to him at the time, 'What's it matter?' I said. I could hardly speak for laughing. But he took it serious. 'I don't like anyone to come prying and peeping like that', he said."

"You're sure it was a motor-bike, not one of these other contrivances on the roads? "

"Quite sure. You could hear the engine and there was only the one light."

"What time did it appear? "

"It was only just dark. Can't have been much more than five. Perhaps a quarter past."

"I see."

"Tell you the truth I'd almost forgotten about it till you brought it up. It wasn't the first time I've been caught when I shouldn't. Good thing it was old Fred Mugger and no one else."

"Why? "

"Oh, everyone knows Fred. Always been the same ever since he was at school. No one takes any notice. But it might have been someone who'd have caused Talk. There's quite enough of that already."

"Someone like Commander Fyfe, for instance?" suggested Carolus.

The jolly loud laugh of Flo filled the room.

"What a thing to say! " she said. "I don't know what put such an idea into your head! 'Pon my word, you have got a wicked mind! I haven't seen him for a week, anyway. He never comes in here. Says he can't leave his wife at night. Oh well, I shall have many a laugh thinking of what you said. I knew there was more than meets the eye about you. I knew that as soon as ever I saw you. Another Milk Stout? Yes, I don't mind."

"You said just now you didn't like Millicent Griggs. I wonder why."

"Because she had a nasty, dirty mind," said Flo with sudden feeling. "I know it if no else did. There was nothing she liked better than getting me to herself and asking questions."

"What sort of questions? "

"Nasty. It would turn you up if I was to tell you. What this man had done and what that one had said. Quite creepy it used to make me feel. I mean, I'm not one for the straight and narrow, but I do bar talking about it in that horrible way. And she was the same with any woman she thought could tell her anything."

11

THERE remained for Carolus only two more interviews in Gladhurst which he regarded, on such facts as he now had, as being of first-rate importance. By a happy chance he was able to kill the two birds with one stone for when he arrived at Crossways to see Miss Flora Griggs he found that Grey was working there that week.

Mrs Bobbin received him in a small sitting-room off the hall, and it seemed that her ire was in no way assuaged by news of the recovery of her sister's jewellery.

"All the jewels on which we could have claimed insurance in any case, and none of the money, on which we can claim nothing. I haven't an idea how much Millicent had with her but it was, as I've told you, usually a large sum. It really is infuriating. I suppose you are no nearer to finding out who was responsible?"

"Not much, I'm afraid. I'm beginning to form a vague idea of how and when and where it may have happened."

"You sound very guarded. I hear you got round that wife of Rumble's. That was an achievement. She's a termagant."

"I found her most obliging. By the way, were your sister's galoshes a brown pair, nearly new, size eight, made by Skilley and Harman?"

"That's right. Have you recovered them, too?"

"The police have them, I think."

"Oh. You've also seen Grazia Vaillant. How did you get on with her?"

"She told me a great deal about her religious views, and other things."

"I suppose butter wouldn't melt in her mouth?"

"She was certainly quite amicably disposed."

"I'm glad. She can be a virago when she's angry."

"That seems to be a common quality among the ladies of Gladhurst."

"And why not? When a woman reaches my age, Mr Deene, she is entitled to her wrath."

"Oh certainly. I'm very anxious to meet Miss Flora Griggs, if it is possible."

"I don't see how she can help you. As I told you she left on the 2.40 bus for Burley. It has come to our knowledge that the police have obtained confirmation of that from the conductor and passengers. Also of the hour of her return. But if you want to meet yet another irate old lady I will introduce you. I ought perhaps to say that Flora has never been intellectually very strong and that the shock of Millicent's death has unsettled her even more. I'll leave you alone with her."

Flora Griggs, when she came into the room, certainly looked wrathful. She was a large woman and had none of Mrs Bobbin's distinguished appearance, but a large-featured face which was lit only by fierce little eyes. She wore unfashionable heavy clothes.

She greeted Carolus civilly enough however, and said she was prepared to tell him anything she could to help him.

"For the murderer must be punished, Mr Deene. 'Whosoever slayeth Cain, vengeance shall be taken on him sevenfold'. Genesis IV, 15," she added in an oracular voice.

"Cain? Why Cain?" Carolus could not resist asking.

"He was Under Protection," explained Flora Griggs.

"You have no suspicion of your own as to who it might be?"

"I am convinced that it can only be one person. Now that we know it was not for 'riches and precious jewels', Second Chronicles XX, 25, we can see the motive as one of hatred. There was only one person who hated Millicent 'with a cruel hatred', Psalm XXV, 19, that is one who, we know too well, is 'wholly given to idolatry', Acts XVII, 16, and plots with papists and conspirators."

"You surely don't mean Miss Vaillant?"

"I mean no other."

"But really, Miss Griggs, I understand that there had been some ill-feeling between these two elderly ladies and that they represented different extremes in a religious controversy. I cannot see how you can suppose that one of them battered the other to death."

"If not with her own hand then by the hand of another."

" But there had been a reconciliation between them."

" I am not deceived by that. ' Grievous words stir up anger ', Proverbs XV, 1, and there had been too many such words in the past years for their anger to abate in a few days."

" Then why do you think your sister went twice to see Miss Vaillant? "

" She did not confide in me but she told me on her return from her visit that we should not for ever suffer, that we should ' be able to stand against the wiles of the devil ', Ephesians VI, 11. It did not seem that she had yet forgiven and I do not believe she had."

Carolus decided to discourage this rather fruitless rhetoric and turn to more practical matters.

" You don't mind if I ask you a few questions about the day of your sister's death, Miss Griggs? "

" I will answer them gladly if it will help you."

" You left the house about half-past two? "

" A little before. I had to catch the 2.40 bus from the village."

" When you left, your sister was resting? "

" Yes. In this room."

" On that very settee, perhaps? "

" Yes. But she did not stay there."

" You mean? "

" She must have gone up to her room to lie down later."

" What makes you say that? "

" Because when I returned and she was missing I looked into that room. The bed had been slept in, or at least laid on."

" Really? Perhaps Naomi had forgotten to make it up that day."

" No. I always help her with the beds. We did my sister's room together."

" Yet when you came back? "

" It was turned back. And something else. I haven't mentioned this to my married sister because I knew it would anger her and there was quite enough to be upset about as it was. But one of the sheets was missing."

"Are you quite sure? "

"Oh quite. It had been pulled from the bed. My sister Mrs Bobbin, as perhaps you've noticed, is somewhat fidgety about details of housekeeping, expenditure and so on. I think she resented my sister Millicent's larger income. She would have been very upset by a missing sheet so I have said nothing about it."

"Did Naomi know of this? "

"I think not. I put the bed cover back as though nothing had happened."

"Thank you, Miss Griggs. That is most valuable information."

"I am glad to tell you anything which will bring the murderer to justice. His 'hands are defiled with blood', Isaiah LIX, 3."

"Now when you left the house that afternoon what was the girl Naomi Chester doing? "

"She was just finishing the washing-up from lunch."

"Did you happen to notice whether she had cleaned the hall that day? "

Flora Griggs made an effort to remember.

"I suppose so. She always does it first. I cannot actually remember seeing her but I think I should have noticed if she had not."

"You made some purchases in Burley? "

"I did. I have given a list of them to the police. They went so far as to question the shopkeepers. Does that mean that they can possibly suppose I had something to do with my sister's death? "

"They have to make these routine enquiries. Then, I understand, you went to the cinema? "

Flora Griggs looked a little confused.

"My sister Millicent disapproved of all places of entertainment," she said, "so I have felt sorry that at the very time of the tragedy I was in a cinema. But I allowed myself an occasional visit. Especially to historical films.

102

That day I saw one called *William the Conqueror* with a most realistic reproduction of the Battle of Hastings."

"I see. And you knew of nothing amiss till you reached home and heard from Mrs Bobbin that Miss Griggs was missing?"

"That's so."

"There is nothing else I want to ask you, Miss Griggs."

"You must succeed!" said Flora Griggs passionately. "'Woe unto the wicked! it shall be ill with him: for the doing of his hands shall be done unto him', Isaiah III, 11."

When Mrs Bobbin returned she found Carolus alone in the little sitting-room.

"Have you learned anything from my sister?"

"I have. Yes. Something most interesting. Now I want to talk to Grey who is working for you."

"Yes. He has just left the firm he worked for and is starting on his own. This is his first job, I believe. We were pleased to help him. He is a very nice young man."

"So I believe."

"It was Naomi Chester who spoke for him, of course. Such a tragedy that. They would be very happily married. I think she persuaded Laddie Grey to give up his job and start on his own, for he has not much initiative."

"And you're helping them?" said Carolus, amused at finding a soft spot in the irascible old lady.

"Actually, there wasn't much that needed doing but Naomi suggested the hall, which can always do with it, and Laddie's apparently a very good painter. He has started on the staircase, which takes a lot of work. Would you like to see him in here?"

"Yes, if I may."

When young Grey came into the room Carolus could see at once why he was so popular. He had that quiet modest charm which is almost bashfulness and appears often in Englishmen who have always worked with their hands. He was not tall but gave an impression of strength

103

behind his gentle eyes and soft speaking voice. There was nothing in the least ingratiating about him but he smiled at Carolus as though he trusted him.

"I won't sit down while I've got these overalls on," he said in reply to a gesture from Carolus.

"You've lived here all your life, Grey?"

"Except for my army service, yes. Dad and Mum are both dead now but Dad had a little shop when he was alive."

"Your wife was from here, too?"

"From over at Breadley—that's about four miles away."

Carolus waited to see if Laddie Grey would say more and after a moment he continued.

"I suppose we were too young," he said. "Everyone said so, anyway. But I was twenty and she was eighteen so I can't really see it. You know about her? I can't understand it. Nothing wrong with her parents as far back as you could go. She was just an ordinary girl, just like other girls, until this happened. Suddenly one day she didn't want to get up, couldn't seem able to do anything for herself or the baby and started thinking she was ill and her brains were all shrivelled up. Then she tried to commit suicide and I sent for the doctor. She's in the Institute over at Wilstone and I go and see her from time to time but she never knows me. The doctors say there's no hope and even if she gets better for a time it will come back."

"Brutal thing, Grey. I'm very, very sorry."

"Thanks. There's nothing to be done about it and I honestly try not to think about it any more. I want to start again with Naomi. We're still young enough, after all. Of course, I shall always feel responsible for the other but her parents are very good about it and they're comfortably off and can see she has what little she needs. I want to marry Naomi if it can be done and I've been to see a lawyer about it."

"I quite understand."

"There's the little girl to think of, too. Naomi thinks

104

the world of her. I don't know what you'll think but I'll tell you what Naomi and I have decided. If these lawyers can't fix it so that we can get married we shall just start as though we were married. I've still got my cottage I had before my wife was taken away and we shall just live there and ——— them, whatever they say. Do you blame us? I mean, what's a church service when they can't give it you and there are three lives to think of? That's what we shall do."

"Mind if I ask you a few questions about the afternoon of the murder?"

Laddie Grey looked rather crestfallen. He had clearly enjoyed expressing his defiance.

"All right. If you think it's any good. I don't see how I can help," he said.

"You were working at Commander Fyfe's that afternoon?"

"S'right. The dining-room."

"Not much before four o'clock someone asked for you on the telephone?"

"So Mrs Fyfe said. When I got to the phone there was no one, so I supposed they'd been cut off. I thought it was the woman who looks after my baby girl."

"You never thought it might be Naomi Chester?"

"No. What would she want to ring me for? I was sure it was Mrs Buxton who looks after Estelle. I thought something might be wrong with the little girl so I left my work a bit early and went on round there."

"And was it Mrs Buxton who had phoned?"

"No. I saw her and Estelle in the street as I was going there so I knew it was all right."

"You didn't ask if she had phoned?"

"Not then, I didn't. Next day or the day after I did and she said certainly she hadn't. So we don't know who it was. I think Mrs Fyfe may have imagined it. She's an invalid and doesn't go out much. She might have got it all wrong."

"What time did you see Naomi Chester?"

"I must have got to her place round about four. But I didn't stay long. We were going to the pictures over at Burley. So I went home, got changed and came back for Naomi. That would have been about five. Then off we went to the pictures."

"Yours is one of several motor-bikes in Gladhurst?"

"Yes. Must be more than a dozen."

"Have any trouble with it?"

"No. Not extra. Now'n again."

"Lights all right?"

"Yes. Certainly. I shouldn't take it out at night without."

"On the bike and on the sidecar?"

"Of course."

"Did you meet anyone before you left for Burley?"

"No. Naomi's mother doesn't get back till late and we didn't see anyone in the village."

"What about in Burley?"

"Not that I remember."

"You went straight to the pictures?"

"Yes."

"Not even a drink?"

"Yes. I expect we had a drink. Usually do."

"Which pub?"

"The Station."

"That's the very large pub that's nearly always crowded?"

"That's it."

"Rather out of your way for the pictures, wasn't it?"

"Bit. We like it."

"Which cinema did you go to?"

"The Gaudeon."

"What was showing?"

"*William the Conqueror.*"

That reply seemed to come very slickly, Carolus thought.

"Look here, Grey. I've told Naomi and I'll tell you.

There's something you're both keeping back. Something one of you has seen or heard. It may not be serious but you should realize how foolish it is in a murder case to hold back even details. Are you trying to protect someone? "

" No." The reply was low and sullen. " I've told you all I know."

" Do you know Dundas Griggs by sight? The old ladies' nephew? "

" No."

" Does Naomi Chester? "

" I expect she does. I've never asked her."

" You make it very difficult for me. I'm going to find out the truth about this, Grey."

" Hope you do. I never wished old Miss Griggs any harm. Nor did Naomi."

" All right," said Carolus. " Have it your own way. I shan't ask you any more."

He left the house soon afterwards feeling depressed and frustrated. He decided to leave Gladhurst at once and return to his own house. His suspicions were turning to conviction, though he had very little concrete evidence behind him.

" The *hell* of a case," he thought. " All in the air and what little comes down to earth is nasty. And only one way to proceed, press and press for the truth till it takes its ugly shape."

" Really, Sir, you look quite done up," said Mrs Stick when he was at last in his own armchair. " I wish you wouldn't overdo it. We shall have you on our hands ill again if you go on like this. You're burning the candle at both ends, what with flying over to that place and doing your schoolwork as well."

" I'm all right. What are you going to give me to eat, Mrs Stick? "

" I've got a nice green pea puray to start with and I'm just going to fry the cruttons for it. Then there's a tiny bit of sole and a fricassay of veal. You'd like a bottle of the Shatto Margo, wouldn't you?"

"Wonderful. You're an angel, Mrs Stick."

"I don't know about an angel but if someone didn't look after you I don't know where you'd be. Poking about with corpses all day—it's not natural. I was only saying to Stick. . . ."

"You're not an angel if you don't bring my dinner."

"All right. I'll be ten minutes because I won't be hurried when it's taken trouble."

"Where's the wine?"

"Here it is, of course. You wanted it shombray, didn't you?"

Carolus forgot the irate old women and the lying young ones for a blissful hour. Then, when he had lit a cigar, he began to make curious half-decipherable notes.

12

BURLEY was an unbeautiful town lying in the midst of a pleasant countryside, like Ashford in Kent or Didcot in Berkshire. It consisted for the most part of streets of medium-sized houses though there were a few more pretentious ones and some slummy little roads of cottages. There was a cattle market and a few uninteresting industries, several Victorian Gothic churches, a fine collection of red-brick chapels, a new town hall and a palatial public lavatory in the town's strategic centre.

Carolus had the address of Dundas Griggs but had been warned that he lived in rooms and was scarcely ever in. When he had asked Mrs Bobbin what was her nephew's occupation she had been rather vague.

"Dundas? Oh he's always busy with schemes of one sort

or another. Knows everyone. Always trying something new. What is called a live wire, I believe, though it doesn't seem to get him anywhere."

Carolus went to his address and found it a solid house called Maitland Villa. His enquiry for Mr Griggs led to a flood of information from a woman with a toupée and glasses.

"No, he hasn't been home since he went out this morning. He's often in about this time but you can never tell with him. He's here, there and everywhere. I tell you where you might find him—round at the Oak Café. There's two or three of them often in there together at teatime. If not, you could try Mr Priestley's office. Or Maugham's the tobacconist's, where he gets his cigarettes and sometimes stops for a chat. Of course, you never know, he may have driven out to Burnside where the new estate's going up because he's been popping over there for something or other. But I think you'll find him in the Oak Café."

"Thank you," said Carolus, making for the gate. But he knew, only too well, the symptoms of tautology.

"If not he's sure to be at Priestley's. He goes in there almost every day. That's the estate agent's just at the bottom of the High Street. If you do miss him there you ask Mr Maugham not three doors away. I don't think he'll have gone out to Burnside."

"No. Well, thank you. . . ."

Carolus had got the gate half open but it was an optimistic gesture.

"Tell you what, though, he might have decided to have his hair cut. If so it'll be at Cronin's on the way to the cattle-market. He was saying he needed a haircut so perhaps that's where he's gone. They don't close till six, so there'd be time for him to have gone to the Oak Café first. That's where you'll find him. It's not very far, if you take this road and keep left at the fork. You'll see it Up— 'Oak Café' on your right. They'll tell you in there if he's been in."

"Thank you," said Carolus, firmly crossing to his car.

"Or else Priestley's office," he heard as he climbed into it. "Or if not . . ."

"Good-bye! " called Carolus cheerfully as he started the engine.

The manageress of the Oak Café was a stately person in black who addressed most of her remarks to the girl in the cash desk.

"Mr Griggs? Isn't that the gentleman who usually sits with Mr Mortimer and Mr Conolly? Yes, I know. He's left, hasn't he? " She turned to Carolus. "He's left," she said.

"Long ago? "

"Was it long ago? " the manageress asked the young lady in the cash desk. "It would be about ten minutes," she said when she had received a reply.

"No idea where he was going? "

"Do *you* know where he was going? " the manageress asked her assistant. "No, I'm afraid I can't say where he was going."

Priestley's, ' the estate agents at the bottom of the High Street ', were scarcely more informative.

"No, not been in here this afternoon, old man," said a tall, thin character in checks who was smoking a pipe which jumped when he talked. "Very often comes in here about this time but he hasn't been in today. I don't know where you'll get hold of him. Tried Maugham's, the tobacconist's? But I shouldn't have thought he'd have gone there without coming here. It's only a few doors away."

Behind the counter of Maugham's was a fair-haired youngish man with a neat moustache.

"Griggs? In here a few minutes ago. In a hurry about something. Bought his cigarettes and was off without waiting to see today's Results. No, I don't know where you'd find him now. Unless he's back at where he lives, Maitland Villa in the Gladhurst Road. I can tell you where he'll almost certainly be after opening time, that's the Saloon Bar of the Chequers. Just opposite the Town Hall."

It was not difficult to find Cronin's, the hairdressers 'on the way to the cattle-market' but an elderly barber at the chair nearest the door, while never ceasing to snip at a small boy's hair, gave Carolus no encouragement.

"I know the gentleman you mean," he said. "If he'd gone anywhere to get his hair cut it would have been here. But we haven't seen him this afternoon. He *may* come in presently, of course. I know he wants a haircut because he told me so in the street yesterday. Hold still. There's a good boy. If you'd like to wait. . . ."

"No, thank you very much. I must go on."

It had occurred to Carolus that rather than pursue Dundas Griggs when he was reasonably sure to find him 'after opening time', he could fill in the remaining hour by trying to confirm Mrs Rumble's rather extraordinary story about Grazia Vaillant. He made for Forster's Stores.

Yet when he was alone with the manager in a small office at the back he suddenly realized how impertinent and irrelevant his enquiry must seem. The manager seemed a kindly type but Carolus felt he must approach the matter with care.

"Look here," he said. "I don't want you to answer my questions if they go against the grain. They'll seem rather cheek to you. The truth is I'm a private detective trying to get at the truth in the matter of an old lady's death at Gladhurst."

"Oh yes, I've read the case."

"I've been at Gladhurst some weeks, on and off, and I must say I find it a hotbed of scandal and malice. One story told me is about a customer of yours, a Miss Vaillant."

"I know Miss Vaillant."

"Someone informs me that Miss Vaillant has started secretly swigging gin. It may be nothing to do with the case but it may have a connection."

"I understand."

"I am told she gets her gin here in single bottles which she takes away more or less surreptitiously."

"I don't see why I shouldn't tell you, though I depend upon you to treat the information as strictly in confidence. It is perfectly true. Horseley's. In oval-shaped bottles which she slips in her shopping bag."

"That's kind of you."

"Tell you something else. The lady who was murdered has been a customer of ours ever since I came to the shop as a boy. She has never been known to order anything alcoholic till about a week before her death. Then she came in and asked me for a bottle of the same, 'for purely medicinal purposes', she said. So I suppose she had started having a little quiet one sometimes, too."

"Looks like it. Thanks awfully and I'll respect your confidence."

"That's all right."

Carolus felt he should give some further explanation.

"You see, if they simply ordered gin or Scotch or anything else there would be nothing to it. Even if they didn't want it themselves it might be for entertaining. But when two elderly women who spend most of their time in activities connected with the parish church suddenly start secretly drinking gin, knocking it back when they're alone, hiding it from their servants, it does seem rather significant."

"Well, there it is. We haven't sold a bottle to Miss Vaillant since the other old lady died, by the way."

"Perhaps that's sobered her. Good-bye and thanks."

On the stroke of six o'clock the Saloon Bar of the Chequers was opened and Carolus walked in, the first customer. An enthusiastic young woman behind the bar served him.

"I'm waiting for Mr Griggs," said Carolus.

"He's *sure* to be in presently," said the barmaid, leaning across towards Carolus.

112

"I don't know him by sight. Will you point him out to me?"

"Of *course* I will. The moment he comes in."

As the room began to fill and Carolus received no sign from the barmaid he grew impatient. At half-past six he asked the girl if Griggs had come in.

"Not yet. I can't understand it. He's always in at this time. Wait a minute. I'll see if anyone knows. Mr Durrell! D'you know where Mr Griggs is?"

Mr Durrell was telling a story and did not like being interrupted.

"Haven't seen him," he said curtly.

"Oh dear, someone must know. He often goes in to Huxley's the bookmaker's to put something on a horse. Have you see him, Mr Huxley?"

"Not today, I haven't."

An informative gentleman broke in.

"Tell you where you're sure to find him. Round at the Queen Charlotte. I know he had to go in there because he was meeting Balchin the builder. Or if not. . . ."

"Thank you," said Carolus. "But I'm not going to start that routine again. I'll wait here till he shows up."

The barmaid blinked reproachfully.

"Mr Hemingway's sure to know," she said. "If *he* says Mr Griggs is round at the Queen Charlotte you can be sure he is."

"Thank you. I'll wait and chance it."

"Mr Powys might know . . . " suggested the barmaid.

"I'll wait."

He was rewarded at last, because at half-past seven a thin jocular man, all neck and wrists, long teeth and chuckles, came in and was told from all sides that Carolus was waiting for him.

"Me? Certainly. Oh yes. My aunt's murder. We'll sit over here. What are you having? I've had a very busy day. You know what it is rushing round?"

"I do indeed," said Carolus, with some feeling.

113

"I heard someone was looking for me. I thought it was in connection with a piece of property I happen to know about. Cheerio. Yes, Aunt Milly's death. Terrible, wasn't it? At her age. Have a cigarette? I don't know. There's an awful lot of violence in the papers. When it happens in a small village it seems worse, somehow. (I'll be with you in a minute, Mr Waugh. I've got that estimate for you.) I was quite upset when I heard about it. . . ."

"When did you hear about it?"

"The murder, you mean? I can't just remember now. Must have been the day after it happened. That's right. My landlady told me. She'd heard on the telephone. Someone had rung me up and she'd taken the message."

"You knew nothing the same night? The Thursday night, I mean?"

"Thursday? No. How could I? No one knew till next morning."

"What time did you get back from Gladhurst that evening?"

"Gladhurst?"

"Gladhurst."

"Oh, that. Yes, I just popped over to see the old ladies. Little proposition I had to suggest. Business. Nothing of consequence."

"And did you see them?"

"No. None of them. But there was a rather extraordinary thing. I reached the house about half-past four. That was the time they liked one to call. As soon as I got in the drive I saw lights on so I thought it was all right. One of them was in, anyway. I hoped it was Millicent. She liked a proposition, bless her. But when I rang the bell, nothing. Not a sound. Not a reply. I rang several times and waited. Nothing at all. Extraordinary thing because they never burnt light when they were out. Very careful about things like that."

"Didn't you try to get in?"

"I walked round, yes. All locked. Back door. Everything. Even the garage. I went away and had a cup of tea in the village. Henson's the bakers do teas there. Then I came back. Must have been a quarter-past five by now."

" It was a dark night, I believe? "

" Pitch black. *And there wasn't a light in the house.* What do you think of that? At four-thirty it's lit up like a Christmas tree. At five-fifteen not a glimmer. Makes you think, doesn't it? "

" It does. How long did you stay there? "

" I thought I might as well ring, in case. I went towards the door and I don't know what made me do it, but before I rang I stood still for a moment. I heard a noise which I recognized at once. Someone was opening the garage doors. I don't know if you've looked round the back of the house but the back door and garages open on to a separate lane."

" Yes. I've seen that."

" There is a way through from the garage into the house. So someone opening the garage doors could have come from inside the house."

" Yes."

" I waited. Listening."

" Where was your car? "

" In the road outside. I couldn't be bothered to get out and open the gates."

" I see. So whoever was in the house or garage might not have known you were there? "

" Almost certainly not. But I know the sound of those garage doors. Have known them for years. I heard them open, then a pause of about three minutes, then they were closed again. I still waited and presently, well down the road, I heard a motor-bike start up."

" Is that all? "

" That's all. I started off for home puzzled but not really worried. Gladhurst has always seemed such a quiet little place. Only next day when I heard the news, I remembered all this. Anything else you want to know? "

115

"Up to you. If you've anything to tell me. . . ."

"No. That's the lot. I've got to run round to the Swan. See a man. Little proposition."

Five minutes after the live wire Dundas Griggs had left the bar, Carolus was amused to see Detective Inspector Champer walk in and ask the barmaid for Griggs.

"He's just this minute gone out. D'you know where he was going, Mr Durrell?"

She had interrupted a longer and duller story than before and received a shorter 'No'. Mr Huxley was no wiser and Mr Hemingway hazarded the Queen Charlotte but Mr Balchin the builder who had talked to him there said he had left half an hour ago to come here, while Mr Powys thought he had gone home.

"That gentleman might be able to tell you," said the barmaid, pointing to Carolus. "He was talking to him."

Detective Inspector Champer unwillingly recognized Carolus and came across.

"Start at Maitland Villa?" asked Carolus.

Champer nodded.

"The Oak Café?"

"Yes."

"Priestley's, the estate agents? Maugham's? Cronin's?"

"There were more than that. Where is the —— now?"

"I shouldn't like to make rash guesses, Inspector. But he told me ten minutes ago that he was going round to the Swan to see a man about a proposition."

Without a word the thick-set policeman pushed his way out of the door.

"So you found Mr Griggs?" said the barmaid keenly to Carolus.

"Yes. He turned up at last."

"You staying here?" she asked, leaning intimately near.

"No. In fact, I'm due home now. Good-night."

But when Carolus had reached his house it was in darkness. The Sticks had gone to bed. There was reproach in every one of his sandwiches.

13

THE Reverend Bonar Waddell looked thoughtful. His finger-tips touched and he stared down at his desk.

"You really feel it necessary to discuss the matter with my curate?" he said at last.

"Not in the least. I want to ask him a few questions."

"Quite. Yes. Naturally. Just so. Of course. To be sure. I understand. I hesitate only because knowing his disposition. . . ."

"What is his disposition?"

"Excellent with boys," said the vicar inevitably. "But diffident, shy, easily upset in adult matters. Between ourselves he is a cause of some anxiety to me. I recognize his value in his own field but I cannot leave much general work to him."

"Sounds like arrested development."

"Arrested? Oh no. I trust nothing of that sort. But he is temperamental. Easily put out. Alarmed by details. I remember one occasion on which our local constabulary in the person of Slatt asked him some questions. Mere trivialities, referring to a dog licence or something. I found him in a highly distressed condition. I had to mediate between him and Slatt as best I could. I seek to impress on you his somewhat excitable character."

"I don't think you need worry. I only want to see him for a moment."

"Then go ahead, my dear chap! Go ahead! Let us put this canker from our midst. If my curate can assist you

117

I feel sure he will be only too glad. I ask you but to approach him with tact."

"Where will I find him?"

"Now? Ah hum. It is his Boys' Club hour. At our village hall. The Griggs Institute is its official designation, presented as it was by the father of the Misses Griggs. There he will be organizing one scarcely knows what."

"Really?"

"The summer camp. Amateur theatricals. Basketball. He is full of ideas. I find myself bound to check his exuberance at times, standing as I do between the parents and him. Last summer he organized an excursion to the coast and the boys' impersonation of Ancient Britons was altogether too realistic. Parents complained of clothes ruined by woad and I received a very unpleasant letter from the Municipal Council. Woad, it was made clear, is no longer sufficient protection for public decency. Several visitors had been outraged by the scene presented. Slipper at once undertook to see that Ancient Britons in future should wear at least bathing slips if not football shorts. I need scarcely say that he had taken no active part in the scene, his rôle being that of a fully clad Boadicea, watching from a chariot."

"That was something," said Carolus encouragingly.

"Unhappily he is not always content with a watching brief. There was an unfortunate incident at their summer camp two years ago. Oh, most unfortunate. I nearly lost one of my best bell-ringers over it. I found myself torn between my loyalty to my curate and my duty as vicar of this parish. It was all very upsetting at the time. However, Slipper's inexhaustible enthusiasm carried the day. With discretion and a little tolerance and the general goodwill which I have always tried to promote the little incident soon became past history. Yes, you go and see my good curate. You will find him busy, I'm sure, but never so deeply involved that he cannot pause to answer questions."

The Reverend Peter Slipper did indeed appear shy as

he disentangled himself from his responsibilities. He was a pale serious young man with a nervous hesitation in his speech. He led Carolus to a small office behind the stage and it seemed as they entered that a sultry hush fell over the mob of youngsters in the main hall. As Carolus entered there had been pandemonium. Now there was no more than a hum of talk.

"It's a Club Night tonight," explained Mr Slipper. "Wednesdays and Saturdays, Club. Mondays and Thursdays, Scouts."

"What is the difference?" asked Carolus curiously.

"*Every* difference. The Boy Scout Movement and the Boys' Club Movement are entirely different things."

"I see. What happens on Tuesdays and Fridays?"

Mr Slipper's face fell.

"Waygooze has those," he said. "He's the choirmaster."

"The boys of Gladhurst seem to have a busy week."

"Even then we haven't enough time, really. They have to pass their tests for badges and there are rehearsals to get in and a thousand activities."

Carolus began to understand the universally-held opinion of Mr Slipper.

"I want, if I may, to ask you a couple of questions," said Carolus.

Mr Slipper started slightly.

"It's about the afternoon on which Miss Griggs was missed."

"Oh, yes."

"Can you remember what you did that day?"

"I was busy all the morning. The D.C. had come over to see me. The District Commissioner, I mean." Seeing Carolus still a little puzzled, as though he thought he was in pre-war Burma, Mr Slipper added, "Scouts, you know. Each county has a County Commissioner and under him are a number of District Commissioners. Ours drove over that day to discuss our Jamboree. He could not stay to lunch, perhaps fortunately, as my digs are scarcely . . ."

"And after lunch?"

"I spent the afternoon preparing for the cookery tests which were to be held that evening. The boys themselves were out borrowing frying-pans and primus stoves but I made the necessary purchases at Jevons's Stores. Young Jevons is one of our Rovers, a ripping chap."

Carolus confessed to himself that his next question was one of sheer human inquisitiveness.

"What purchases?" he asked.

"They pass out on a pancake," explained Mr Slipper rather obscurely. "No eggs, of course. Flour, milk, frying-fat. They have to eat them afterwards. That's the test. Those without indigestion get badges."

"Very appropriate. So you purchased the ingredients?"

"Yes."

"What time do you think you reached Jevons's Stores?"

"I imagine in the region of 3.45."

"Whom did you meet?"

"Now let me see. Oh yes. Our Churchwarden. Commander Fyfe."

"Was he alone?"

"Well, as it happens he had stopped for a moment to address a few words to . . . a parishioner."

"You mean Flo?" asked Carolus rather brutally.

Mr Slipper nodded.

"It wasn't more than a minute. Just passing the time of day . . ." he explained eagerly.

"Of course. Anyway, I like Flo. Don't you?"

"Oh, I scarcely . . . indeed I have never . . . I do not criticize . . . It's a matter for the vicar."

"Who else appeared in the village street?"

"Naomi Chester. I saw her pass while I was in the Stores. She seemed in a great hurry."

"You don't remember anyone else?"

"No. I daresay there were others. I was, of course, preoccupied. These cookery tests! Last year the boys got rather excited and upset some hot fat. Lawrence Tilley's hand was rather badly burnt. In fact he couldn't use it for some days. I had a great deal on my mind."

" "You have a motor-cycle, Mr Slipper? "

" A Lambretta, yes."

" But you did not use it that afternoon? "

" No. I was on foot. My digs, the stores and this hall are all within a few hundred yards of one another."

" Did you see Rumble or Mugger? "

" I don't remember seeing either. When I had made my purchases I went back to my digs to tea then came round here at five o'clock for the tests. We had seven passes."

" I congratulate you. And I'm most grateful for your patience in answering my questions. I won't interrupt your Club Night any further."

As he left the hall the din that rose behind him was like that of a wild beasts' cage at feeding time.

Carolus intended leaving at once for Newminster but as he passed the Black Horse he saw Mugger emerging and stopped his car. Mugger, tall and angular in the light thrown by the bulb over the inn sign, did not look furtive. When he spoke it was in his usual serious tones.

" Evening, Mugger," said Carolus.

" I can't stop now," said Mugger. " I've got one waiting for me out by the cricket field."

" I shan't delay you long," promised Carolus.

" Better not, because I don't want to miss this one. Just right she is, if you know what I mean."

" Yes, yes. I wanted to ask you about a sheet."

Nothing was changed in Mugger's posture or expression.

" What sort of sheet? " he asked.

" Come now, Mugger. Don't let's waste time and words. You don't suppose I meant a sheet of paper or part of the rigging of a ship. You know exactly which sheet."

" I don't know what you're talking about. And what's more I shall have to hurry. They won't wait all night."

" Then let's be explicit. I haven't made myself difficult about the sum of money. . . ."

"There was no money," sighed Mugger, but almost mechanically.

"So why not trust my discretion over this?"

"What d'you want to know?"

"Where you found it."

"Up in the loft of the furnace room, of course. With the other things."

"*With* them?"

"Well, just beside. It was crumpled up and stuffed into a box."

"Blood-stained?"

"Yes."

"What on earth induced you to move it, Mugger?"

"Well, a sheet's a sheet, nowadays."

"I find you very hard to understand. You leave the jewellery and take a sheet."

"The sheet could be washed, couldn't it? There'd be nothing to say where it come from. But jools, that's different. The police can trace them. Before I knew where I was I'd be up for murdering the old lady which I never done."

"I see. Where's the sheet now?"

"Never mind that. It's been washed. You'd never know it from any other, now. And if you were to go and say anything I should know nothing about it. Never seen a sheet. Never heard of one. Never spoke to you about it. And no one would know any different."

"It was badly blood-stained?"

"Very badly. Horrible in fact. Now I can't wait any longer. I can't afford to miss one like this."

He strode away, his long shanks and thin body exaggerated by the yellow overhead light.

Carolus was about to drive on when he saw Slatt. It seemed that the policeman had been observing him during his conversation with Mugger and now approached.

"You know what the Inspector told you, don't you?" he said as though he were addressing a small and naughty

122

boy. "You've no business to be nosing round with what doesn't concern you. I should very much like to know what you were asking Mugger."

"Really? Perhaps Mugger will tell you."

"I'm surprised you encourage him," said Slatt. "He gives more trouble than all the rest of the village put together. I hear you've been round to see Miss Vaillant, too. I can't see how she can concern you. What I'm always afraid of is a burglary there. She's all on her own and the house is full of valuables. Antiques and that."

"I know. There's a landscape by Constable."

"Police Officer!" said Slatt, so alert for the offensive word that he could not wait to study niceties of meaning.

"I'm always forgetting," said Carolus. "A landscape by Police Officer. But I shouldn't have thought there was much danger of burglary in a place like this."

"If there can be murder there can be burglary," said Slatt darkly.

"What really seems to distinguish your village is the enmity between its inhabitants. Particularly the older ones."

"You don't know the half of it," said Slatt. "There's the three old sisters to start with. There was no love lost among them. I've heard that Mrs Bobbin could lay her tongue to some terrible language when she was put out with the one that's been done for. The other one would shout the Old Testament at both of them. Proper slanging match. That's only what I hear, though."

"Of course."

"Then the vicar's wife's not much better. You should have heard her going on about the Miss Griggses according to what they tell me. Talk about words! Miss Vaillant's different. She's sweet as sugar till suddenly she's raging like a wild cat. Funny, isn't it? Then look at Mrs Rumble!"

Carolus put in a mild defence of the sexton's wife.

"You don't know her, that's all I can say," returned

Slatt. "She's got a wicked temper. Commander Fyfe's wife's just the same, only she's laid up half the time. They say you can hear her shouting at him from two doors away. Then what about Mrs Pinton?"

"I don't know her."

"She's the doctor's wife. I've seen her lose her temper as much as any of them. As for them up at what they call Hellfire Corner—well!"

"I believe Mugger's married?"

"There's another one! I thought she was going for me the other morning when I had to ask her something. She was out the back, doing her washing."

"No woman likes a man to watch that."

"Perhaps that's what upset her. She seemed to have a lot of it. And of course with Mugger out poaching at night there was blood on things. But it wasn't that. It was me seeing her without one of these washing machines all the women have."

"You mean she was using an old-fashioned cop . . . police officer?"

Slatt seemed not to notice this gaffe.

"Turned on me something wicked, she did. What business had I got coming out to her back yard? You're right in what you say about this village. When George Larkin's wife was alive she was no better. It was always my belief that she knew about him and Miss Griggs going off together when they were young and never forgave him for it. She never liked the old ladies, anyway, and didn't want young Bill to have anything to do with them."

"Yet I understand that Miss Griggs has remembered both the Larkins in her will."

"That's the funny part of it. She's left Bill just as much as his father and he was nothing to do with her. Of course, after George Larkin's wife died, young Bill used to go up and see the old lady. They're very deep, those Larkins. Both of them. You never know where you are with them."

Suddenly Slatt became alert.

"They're coming out of the Griggs Institute," he said. "All those young devils'll be raising Cain in the street if I don't get down there."

"They don't seem to be making much noise," said Carolus.

"It's not that. They get all over the place laughing and talking. If I'm not there they think they can do what they like."

"You'd better go and show them they can't," said Carolus and Slatt, unconscious of irony, pushed his cycle away.

Carolus decided to have a last drink in the Black Horse before leaving for home, and found himself, as on his first night, beside the informative Mr Lovibond.

"You didn't tell me you were finding out about the murder when we had our chat before," said Lovibond. "Still, I don't suppose you want to tell your business to everyone, especially when it's something of that sort. It was young Laddie Grey told me. One of the nicest chaps you could wish to meet. He came in my shop the other day to buy a bulb for his motor-bike. I think I told you I keep a little electric shop down the road. Yes, young Laddie came in and mentioned to me that you'd been asking him questions."

"Was it a headlight bulb he wanted?" asked Carolus casually.

"No. It was for the light on his sidecar, because I saw him fix it in. So you've been round asking everyone, have you?"

"Yes. I seem to have met a good many of the inhabitants of Gladhurst."

"Talked to old Flo yet?"

"I have met her. Yes."

"She's a Character, isn't she? You never know who you'll see her with next. There's a story going round about her and Fyfe who lives up at The Fairway. I shouldn't be surprised, mind you. It wouldn't be the first married man, not by a long way. But she doesn't mean anyone any harm. It's only the wives get a bit upset when stories get back to them. Not that my old woman would bother. As long as I don't forget her light ale when I go home at night she never says a word."

" That's good."

" Look at old George Larkin watching the clock. He knows Slatt's outside holding his watch. He'll start shouting ' Time! ' in a minute."

Carolus decided to leave before the split-second ejection by synchronized watches had taken place.

14

CAROLUS was free for the following week-end and wanted to spend it in Gladhurst. But before arranging this he approached the headmaster for formal leave of absence, a gesture of courtesy which he would not omit.

He found an opportunity of speaking to Mr Gorringer on the Wednesday afternoon, for a lecturer was due to address the school on Tanganyika (with lantern slides), and afternoon classes were therefore cancelled. The lecturer was late and the Headmaster paced impatiently before the moderately-sized room known as the Great Hall in which the school's 250 boys were gathered.

" Ah Deene, you find me in a frame of mind by no means equable. If there is a fault to me unforgivable it is that of unpunctuality. Our lecturer is already ten minutes late."

" The fog, perhaps."

" Fog? It was his duty to provide against all climatic exigencies. His fee is twelve guineas, which, though it includes expenses, seems to be adequate."

"I wonder what his agent stings him, poor devil," said Carolus.

"That, my dear Deene, is not our affair. Thirteen minutes. The boys will grow restless shortly."

"I want to be away this week-end, headmaster."

"Again? Really Deene, you are quite deserting us. Have you no wish to see our match against St Hildegarde's? And perhaps you have forgotten that the Dean of Bodmin is preaching in the School Chapel on Sunday?"

"It's rather an urgent matter. I feel if I can stay a weekend among these people at Gladhurst I can get the thing cleared up for good. It's the way one knows a village like that."

"At least I respect your candour, Deene, in telling me the reason you wish to elude us again. That much I appreciate. But I could have wished that the promise of a hardfought football match, together with the celebrated eloquence of the Dean of Bodmin . . . However, I will not stand in your way. It shall never be said that I adopt a restrictive or a carping attitude towards my staff. You may go and I hope will return with all mysteries elucidated."

"Thank you."

"Dear me. A full quarter of an hour late. I shall be constrained to send the boys back to their classrooms and abandon all thought of the lecture, for which, fortunately, the fee has not yet been paid. So we are to hear shortly the identity of this brutal murderer at Gladhurst? I trust you will make me among the first to hear details? I must tell you a witticism of my wife's on that subject. She . . . Ah, but unless I mistake me this is our lecturer at last. . . ."

The headmaster hurried forward and Carolus, with a sigh, sat to see lantern slides of Tanganyika. These consisted largely of hefty negroes in postures which, the lecturer assured his audience, were those of a native dance.

When Saturday came, Carolus set off immediately after morning school, having a delightful sense of escape. It was not often he allowed himself a night away from Newminster during term-time but the reason he had given to the headmaster in this case was a genuine one. He believed that a small thing like going to bed and waking up in Gladhurst, spending Saturday night in the pub and Sunday morning in the church, being for a few hours one of the village inhabitants, might make all the difference to his understanding of them. And on that depended the whole case.

His first call was at the vicarage. Mrs Waddell opened the door and spoke with something like a note of triumph.

" My husband's preparing his sermon for tomorrow and cannot possibly be disturbed. My daughter's out on her bike."

" That's all right," said Carolus blandly. " It was you I hoped to find at home, Mrs Waddell."

She gave him a short defiant stare, then said: " Come in, then."

" I must really apologize for troubling you again," said Carolus. " You'll think I'm an awful idiot. The thing is, I'm trying to work out a complete timetable for everyone's movements after two-thirty that day and I find I have a blank in yours."

" It sounds like a sort of game," said Mrs Waddell grimly.

" Not really. It's rather important. You explained to me that you had your Mother's Meeting from four to six, I think. That was at the Griggs Institute, perhaps? "

" It was."

" I see. But it's only about five minutes from here and your daughter remembers you returning at 6.45 or more. It is that three-quarters of an hour I want to fill in."

" I find the query somewhat impertinent, Mr Deene, but in order not to be badgered with further questions I will tell you at once. The Scouts were holding their

Cookery Tests at the Institute. I watched for a time to see that everything was all right. Last year there was nearly a nasty accident."

"Did you speak to Mr Slipper?"

"No. He hates being interrupted while he is with his boys. I just stood in the shadows at the back for a while, then came away."

"No one saw you?"

"I shouldn't think so. They were furiously concentrated on their pancakes."

"Thank you, Mrs Waddell. I needn't take any more of your time."

On his way round to Commander Fyfe's he caught a glimpse of a somewhat bizarre group. Mr Slipper was in the full uniform of a Scoutmaster and with him were several sturdy Rovers with a laden pushcart. Carolus sighed. It was an excellent thing, the Boy Scout Movement, but why oh why did it encourage grown men whose physiques could not stand the test to wear this uniform? For healthy youngsters, splendid, but for curates no longer youthful, with angularities like Mr Slipper's, fatal. Those blue knees! But he waved a greeting to the curate and drove on towards The Fairway.

Fortunately he found himself stopped in the road and without any explanation Fyfe climbed in beside him.

"The very man I want to see!" he said. "Most extraordinary thing. Could we drive on a little? Out of the village perhaps?"

When they had reached a fairly open stretch of road about a mile away, Fyfe dropped his voice.

"It's Dundas Griggs," he said. "He guessed it was I who told you he was over here."

"How did he guess that?"

"Because he saw me when he was driving his Vauxhall and stopped."

"You didn't tell me."

"So many strange things happened that day. I couldn't

129

tell you them all. I've seen him over here before. He goes to call on the old ladies; then we usually meet at the Black Horse in the evening. Saloon bar, of course. It's quiet there. He told me that afternoon he had a little proposition for me."

"Quite a Euclidian, Mr Griggs."

"I beg your pardon? Oh. Who is this coming down the road on a bicycle? You see you never know here."

"You were telling me about that afternoon."

"Yes. Arranged to meet for a drink later. I told you. I was able to leave the house for a while. My gardener and his wife . . . television. . . ."

"Yes. Yes."

"Then the really extraordinary thing happened. I can't think why I didn't tell you before. *Griggs never turned up.* I waited an hour for him. Not a sign. Never came. What do you think of that?"

"Very bad manners."

"Manners? But don't you see, man? He's the nephew of the murdered woman and on the night of her death he fails to keep an appointment! Doesn't it strike you as sinister?"

"Not necessarily."

"Then today. Over here again. Remonstrating with me for having told you he was in Gladhurst that day. Says *he* doesn't want to get mixed up in the thing. He was quite annoyed. I consider that highly significant."

Carolus proposed to drop Commander Fyfe at his home but he grew somewhat nervous at the prospect.

"No! Don't stop right outside. You never know. It doesn't do in a place like this. Leave me by the Griggs Institute. I'll walk home."

At the Black Horse he found George Larkin alone, for the doors had only just been opened.

"I wonder if you could let me have a room for tonight?" asked Carolus.

"We don't Do rooms."

"Oh. Pity."

130

" I'll ask Mrs Crutch who looks after that side of it. She might be able to."

He returned after a few minutes.

" She says there *is* a room. But you mustn't expect too much. It's clean and that and she'll air the bed. That's all."

" What more could one want? "

" Some expect a lot."

" I'll bring my bag in."

" All right. Bill will take it up. You'll want something to eat presently, I suppose? "

" Whatever's easy."

Carolus ordered a drink and after it was poured the innkeeper returned to his static contemplation of the wall opposite, expressionless solidity on his face. It was ten minutes before the first of his Saturday night customers came in.

This was Rumble, looking particularly pleased with himself. His gnomish head on his stocky body suggested one of Disney's seven dwarfs. He accepted a pint from Carolus and at once began to congratulate him.

" I've never seen anything like it! " he said admiringly. " There you was in the kitchen drinking tea. It's as much as I dare do to sit in that chair which is supposed to have belonged to her father. However did you manage it? "

" I've yet to see all this bad temper your wife is credited with."

" Bad temper? You try living with her. Anyway, she'll be in presently and you can see for yourself. I've got something to tell you, though. Might be of some help to you. See, Mrs Bobbin called me into the hall today to help put the furniture back now that Laddie Grey's finished painting in there. Miss Flora was out and I didn't know where she'd gone but while I was still indoors she came storming in. I've never seen her anything like it. Firing texts off at the top of her voice. It appears she had been to Miss Vaillant's."

"What sort of texts?"

"All about the Wicked. 'The wicked laid a snare for me', she says from Psalms. 'A woman with the attire of an harlot and wily at heart', from Proverbs, I think it was. But we've had all this before about Miss Vaillant. It was something else made me think."

"Yes?"

"She started on about 'be not among wine-bibbers', and causing strong wine to be poured, and strong drink is raging, and all that. It sounded to me as though somebody had offered her a nip and she'd turned up her nose at it. What do you say?"

"I didn't hear it," said Carolus guardedly.

"I thought you'd like to know, anyway. This pub soon gets filled up on a Saturday, doesn't it?"

The bar was certainly growing crowded. When Flo came in and was greeted on all sides, there seemed to be a hilarious atmosphere.

"*There* you are!" said Flo to Carolus as though they were old friends. "You haven't taken me out in that car of yours yet, have you? There's a promise for you! Perhaps you're waiting for the nice weather. It reminds me of a fellow I knew once who used to say it was no good going out except in the Spring. What an idea! I asked him what he did all the rest of the year. Not that I minded, because he wasn't the only pebble on the beach. We shall all start singing presently so I don't know what you'll say about that. Saturday night, after all."

Carolus saw Mr Lovibond making his way across and knowing that the little electrician regarded him as a protégé he made room for him and invited him to drink.

"The vicar will be in presently," said Lovibond surprisingly. "Always comes in for a few minutes on Saturday evening."

And sure enough before eight o'clock, complete with clerical collar and bland smile the Reverend Bonar Waddell was amongst them.

"I see you are quite an habitué," he said to Carolus. "Ah well, there's no harm in a little cheerfulness at the end of a week. I myself am in a slightly more difficult situation. On the one hand many of the most sincere and loyal members of my congregation, including the landlord himself, are customers here and appreciate my presence for a short time. On the other hand many no less earnest folk in the parish regard strong drink as the devil's potion and a public house as a place of evil."

"So how do you manage?" asked Carolus, fascinated as usual by the delicate balances which Mr Waddell held in his hand.

The vicar smiled.

"I come here, as you see, but only for a short time on Saturday. And I invariably order for myself a lemonade."

"Very ingenious."

The vicar looked more grave.

"But tell me," he said. "How go your investigations?"

"It's a complicated case."

"That's just what we all thought at first it was *not*. Brutal, predatory, savage, cowardly, it seemed but of almost primitive simplicity. Now that we know the motive was not mere robbery it wears another complexion."

"Yes. It seems to bring it home to the village, doesn't it?"

The vicar looked anxious.

"There are times when I almost wonder whether it would not be better left a mystery, Mr Deene," he said. "I see, of course, that 'vengeance is mine', that such a crime cries out for it, but then I think, too, that revelation will mean more bloodshed, more suffering by those perhaps not directly concerned. I am torn in my hopes and sympathies. Ah well, I must greet some of these good people. Good evening, Frank. Good evening, Mugger. Ah, Rumble. Er hum, good evening, Flo. I see you well, Mrs Rumble? That's right. Full chime of bells tomorrow, Gidley? Splendid. Ah, Laddie. And Bill. Nice to see you all. No, no thank you. I've had my allowance. I must be making my way homewards. Good-night, Larkin. Good-night to you, Deene. Good-night, all! Good-night! "

Though he went out amid the smiles of the customers, the vicar's departure seemed to remove a little constraint from the assembly.

"Well now we can have a sing-song," said Flo exuberantly. "Come on, Mrs Chester! You're not going to sit there like a mute, I can tell you. We know what you can do when you get started, can't she, Mr Lovibond? It reminds me of the married couple that were worried because . . ."

"Now, Flo."

"All right, Mr Larkin. I wasn't going to say a word. Only we must have a bit of a sing if it's only to make the Sheriff wild. He's standing outside already looking at his watch."

Carolus found himself wedged in a corner with Mrs Rumble.

"Is that right you're staying here tonight?" she asked.

"Yes. I thought . . ."

"You know she still hasn't taken a drop. Funny, isn't it? Mind you, I don't know what happened this afternoon when that Flora Griggs got there. I hope she's not as bad as the other one. But anyway, up to then she hadn't touched it. Must have given her a nasty shock, that other."

"Perhaps that was it."

"Now, Rumble, don't you hang round here because you've had one pint off the gentleman and I'll see he doesn't buy you any more. You've had enough already by the looks of it."

"I haven't. . . ."

"Now don't keep on or I shall Tell you. You go and talk to old Mugger, he's more your mark."

It seemed but a few minutes after that when George Larkin was shouting "Time!" and the exodus was made in good order and swiftly under the eye of Slatt.

134

Carolus went into the open air with the rest and found himself standing almost alone with a somewhat argumentative man of large proportions.

"What I say is," said this individual, "I'm one of the few blacksmiths left working a forge."

"I daresay," said Carolus.

"And it's an old trade and a good one."

"It's both, yes."

Slatt was approaching.

"A man who can work with iron, *is* a man," said the blacksmith.

"You're right," said Carolus. "You know what Kipling says:

'*Gold is for the mistress—silver for the maid!*
Copper for the craftsman cunning at his trade.'"

"What did you say?" asked Slatt.

"Sorry," returned Carolus.

"*Police officer for the craftsman, cunning at his trade.*
'*Good!' said the Baron, sitting in his hall,*
'*But Iron—Cold Iron—is master of them all!'*"

"That's right," said the blacksmith.

Carolus bade them both good-night and joined the Larkins, father and son, in a plentiful cold meal. He found that his bedroom overlooked the lower part of the village and against a cold moonlit sky he could see the silhouette of the church tower.

15

CAROLUS was awakened by a loud persistent knocking on his door before it was light. There is always something slightly macabre about knocking like this, forceful, unhurried, continuous. Carolus thought of Macbeth and how well Shakespeare had used that sound to introduce the horrible bloodstained humour with which he heightened the effects of his tragedies.

" Come in! " he shouted, switching on the light.

George Larkin entered.

" There's someone downstairs wants to see you. Urgent."

How typical of him not to say who it was when he knew perfectly well.

" All right. I'll be down in a few minutes."

He dressed as quickly as he could, washing in cold water in the china bowl on the mahogany stand. He hurried downstairs and in the Larkins' little sitting-room found Mrs Rumble.

He was accustomed to seeing her long plain face set in lines of ferocity. Now she looked startled and anxious.

" Come outside a minute," she said. " I want to speak to you."

Carolus followed her to the inn yard.

" I don't know whether I done right. I thought once they get in you'll never be able to find out anything. So I've come to tell you first. She's dead."

" Miss Vaillant? " Carolus scarcely needed to ask.

" Yes. Dead as a doornail. Slumped across the settee with an expression on her face as though she'd like to kill you."

" But you ought to have gone to the police."

" I am going. But you may as well have a look first. You might find something. They'll never let you near when they get there. Come on quick and no one will be the wiser."

It was altogether too tempting. Carolus realized that the consequences might be serious but he had to chance that.

They drove swiftly to the Old Vicarage.

" Put your car over there as though you were in church for early Communion and no one will notice it. There will be several there. That's it. Now we go in round the back."

Mrs Rumble had her key of the back door and admitted them.

" Was this locked? " asked Carolus.

" Oh yes, so was the front. This way."

There certainly was an expression of apoplectic anger on the face of Grazia Vaillant where she lay twisted half across the settee. It was as though she knew herself to be dying and instead of commending her soul to God, as the expression used to be, she was angry at being subjected to the indignity and uncertainty of death. The eyes were wide open in a fixed indignant gaze and the hands were twisted as though she had suffered convulsive movements.

" Quite cold, of course? "

" Yes. Must have been dead for hours. From yesterday evening very likely."

Miss Vaillant's bag was open beside her on the floor and she was dressed in one of her curious coarse outfits with large jewellery, the whole suggesting a Balkan peasant woman. The curtains had been drawn close and it was by electric light that Carolus and Mrs Rumble stared at her.

" Do you think she was murdered? " asked Mrs Rumble.

" How can we possibly know till after the doctor's report? "

" I suppose not. I mean, she looks as though she's been murdered, doesn't she? "

" She looks very distressing. Which is the cupboard you told me about of which you have a key? "

"This one," said Mrs Rumble and opened a little cupboard on one side of the sideboard.

"Well! That's a funny thing," she said. "There was a bottle nearly a third full here yesterday. I told you she hadn't touched it since the other one died. Now it's gone, bottle and all."

Carolus went to the back door and saw the old well which Mrs Rumble had mentioned. It was one of those deep narrow shafts which drop darkly down to a just visible black surface of water.

"That's where she must have thrown the bottle like she did all the other ones."

They returned to the room where Miss Vaillant's body lay and Carolus looked down on it unhappily.

"What did she carry in her bag?" he asked. "No! Don't touch it! Let me look in."

With a handkerchief over his finger Carolus gingerly turned over the contents.

"About ten pounds in money," he said. "Would that be usual?"

"Just about. She didn't draw a lot at a time. She liked paying things by cheque."

"There's a tube of Minerval. They're very powerful tranquillizers. On Doctor's prescription only. Did she take many?"

"I bought that tube new for her a week ago. She must have been taking them since then. In fact I know she has because I happened to notice yesterday there was only two left."

"It's empty now," said Carolus. "If she took the lot in one go it could have killed her."

"She couldn't have done that, could she? There was nothing wrong when I left yesterday afternoon. In fact she was quite excited about getting a statue on the altar of the side chapel. It seems now Miss Griggs is Gone the vicar agreed. Still, you never know."

"You're quite sure about the gin?"

"Certain. I saw it only yesterday."

" You said she drank lime juice with it? "

Mrs Rumble stooped.

" Yes and that's Gone Down, too. She must have had a good old time after I'd gone yesterday."

" What about the glass? "

" If she threw the bottle away she washed the glass up. You may be sure of that. Many's the time I've come in in the morning and found just the one glass in the sink. She thought she fooled me with that but I knew better. I'll go and see if there's one now."

" Don't touch it," warned Carolus.

Mrs Rumble returned to say yes of course there was. She had known there would be.

Carolus made a quick tour of the house. He found the front door bolted, all the windows with their catches across and nothing forced anywhere. It would seem that if anyone entered last night it was with a key of the back door.

Then once again he looked round the room in which the dead woman lay. On the table, beside the settee across which she sprawled, were several lurid-looking tracts. The title of the top one intrigued him:

Satan Raises his Glass.

It was issued by the All-World League of Absolute Abstainers. Another, scarcely less ostentatious, was called:

There's an Inn-Sign on the Road to Hell

But beneath these two were tracts dealing with Missions to Hindus, Jews and Mohammedans and aids to the study of the Old Testament. They were all fresh-looking and had surely come from the ample stock kept by Flora Griggs.

Carolus looked carefully for anything else which might reveal events or visitors last night. Miss Vaillant's glasses were beside the tracts so no doubt she had examined them with some mirth. The room had been carefully dusted, a

139

tribute to Mrs Rumble, and only the experts would know whether there were fingerprints of anyone but the dead woman and her housekeeper.

"Was Miss Flora Griggs here yesterday?" Carolus asked Mrs Rumble.

"Yes. She was here when I left. But I'll tell you about that another time. There isn't a minute now because I must phone the police."

"What time did you leave?"

"Just after four. I went off to do my shopping."

"Did you meet anyone in the village?"

"I'll tell you all that later when I've had time to think. I *did* see Naomi Chester, I remember, and Commander Fyfe was there too."

A bell began to chime in the church tower across the road.

"That's Early Service," said Mrs Rumble, forgetting the less evangelical terms which Miss Vaillant had taught her. "You better pop across there and no one will know any different. I'll ring the police as though I'd just come. You can go out the back way and mind no one sees you."

When Carolus came out of the church half an hour later there was great activity in front of the Old Vicarage. Slatt was making a show of directing traffic and moving on anyone who hesitated near the house. Several police cars were drawn up and there seemed to be much coming and going through the front door, which Mrs Rumble, doubtless, had opened.

Carolus stood beside his car for a moment and was surprised to see Champer hurrying across.

"I believe you knew about this," he said aggressively.

"What?" asked Carolus with far too much innocence.

"I tell you again, if I catch you interfering in any way I'll charge you. There are going to be no amateur detective tricks when I'm investigating."

"Something happened?" asked Carolus.

Champer made a sound between a spit and a cough and stumped away.

The news had preceded Carolus to the Black Horse but did not seem to impair the appetites of the Larkins. Carolus found himself breaking all precedents by eating bacon and eggs.

"Do you think she was done for?" asked George. "Or did for herself? Or died natural?"

"I know no more than you till the inquest and we hear medical evidence."

"They say she looked like Dracula," said Bill Larkin.

Carolus remained silent.

There was a call just then from Mrs Bobbin asking Carolus to go up to the house. He wondered for a moment how she knew he was staying the night at the Black Horse, then remembered Rumble.

The old lady stood with her usual uprightness and looked Carolus in the eyes.

"This has dreadfully upset my sister Flora, Mr Deene. I feel inclined to send for a doctor. She is quite beside herself."

"I'm sorry."

"You see, she called to see Grazia Vaillant yesterday afternoon."

"I know."

"How do you know?"

"It is common knowledge," said Carolus evasively.

"She returned in a state of great indignation. My sisters, as I think I have told you, were strict teetotallers. It appears that Grazia Vaillant not only pressed poor Flora to drink but said that during those two last visits to her which Millicent made, Millicent had drunk with her. Flora came back to me *speechless* with indignation."

"Is that quite the right word?"

"No. But very, very angry. And now Grazia Vaillant is dead."

"So I have heard."

"Mr Deene, do you think my sister was the last person to see her alive?"

"I think it very likely."

141

"Then . . . but it is monstrous. If Grazia Vaillant did not die naturally, or commit suicide, some suspicion might attach to Flora?"

"I don't know the workings of the police mind. I think in any case we should wait to hear the cause of death when it has been established. The woman may have had a heart attack."

"It's so extraordinary after the other. You are not very reassuring, Mr Deene."

"No. I'm afraid I can't be in this matter. It has a very ugly look."

"You say it is generally known that my sister called at the Old Vicarage?"

"I understand she left some religious tracts there."

"Did she? Oh!" For a moment Mrs Bobbin seemed crestfallen, then she said: "But she might have given them to Grazia Vaillant at any time."

"I think, Mrs Bobbin, if you will permit me to say so, you are suggesting something rather dangerous. Your sister certainly called there, there are probably witnesses. It would be most unwise to attempt to conceal it, in my view."

"You may be right. But I hope these wretched policemen don't come here to bother her, at least till she has got over the shock."

"I shouldn't count on that," said Carolus as he took his leave.

Moreover he was right. He met Champer at the gate.

"Well, Inspector, we meet again," he said brightly. But the policeman pushed by.

At about mid-day Carolus sat on a comfortable grave-stone in the village churchyard waiting for the general dispersal of the congregation. In front of him he could see the plain oval-topped affair already erected 'To the Memory of Albert Chilling'. Carolus remembered that, but for the keen observation of Rumble, Millicent Griggs's body might still be deep there in the earth and the Gladhurst Case have been no more than that of another old lady disappearing from her usual orbit.

In the church he could hear the choir celebrating the Greatest Mystery of the Universe in a rollicking tune:

> *Three in One and One in Three*
> *Rulers of the Earth and Sea*

sang the choir cheerily because the service was nearly over and soon they would be free, the men to seek the Black Horse, the boys for an hour's smoke before Sunday dinner.

Carolus was interested to see how the congregation would take the new tragedy in the village. But when they began to emerge it was difficult to know what its impact had been. Was there an extra solemnity? Or did he imagine that among those groups with bowed heads and solemn gait the death of Grazia Vaillant was the sole topic? Did they think there was some mystery about it? Or were they persuading themselves it was from natural causes?

The choir came out of the vestry door in a talkative stream. Certainly these youngsters were not much troubled by the death of another old lady.

Then came Mr Slipper in hot argument with a tall grizzled man whom Carolus knew to be Waygooze the Organist and Choirmaster. On Slipper's face was a look of petulant, rather childish annoyance.

" It does not seem much of a concession to ask," he said. " It is only Tuesday nights that I want Stanley. You can have him on Fridays."

" You've already got four nights a week for your activities, Mr Slipper," said Waygooze solemnly. " I'm not going to have the boys interfered with on Tuesdays. They come to choir practice then."

" I don't want them. I've explained to you it's just one boy, Stanley Rogers, to help me get the Institute in order.

143

Unless you'd like him and Cyril Lipscombe to do it turn and turn about? They could do half an hour with you then come down to the Institute."

"And what do you think would happen to the new Magnify Cat if I once started letting them go down whenever they liked? No, Mr Slipper. I'm sorry. Stanley comes to choir practice on Tuesdays and Fridays. You'll have to find someone else for your little job."

The vicar caught them up.

"Now what are you two good people discussing? Ah, yes. Choir practice. The Institute. But I think that *today*, on this day of great personal loss to us all and perhaps even more troubles for our little community, we should forget our personal differences. I've no doubt some way out can be found. Let us forget it for the present."

When Carolus reached the Black Horse he found that festive occasion known through the week as 'Sunday dinner-time' was in full swing. Sunday suits were stiff and shiny, vegetables dug that morning were on the handlebars of bicycles outside the pub, ale was freely poured and darts were thrown. The conversation today turned on the second sudden death in Gladhurst and most of those present had something to say about it.

Flo led the discussion.

"You can't call old Griggs's anything *but* murder," she said. "But I can't see what you make a mystery of this for. The poor old cow had a drop too much, passed out and there you are. Well, we've all got to Go some day so I don't see what all the fuss is about. It reminds me of a fellow I used to go on the back of his motor-bike with, and whenever we went round the corner on the wrong side he'd say, 'No one's going to live for ever, you know' and laugh till he could hardly steer. He used to take me out to an old straw stack and I'd come away covered with chaff, but I didn't mind."

"I don't believe it was an accident," said Mr Lovibond. "I believe one man did for both of them. Just because he did it different ways—that's nothing. It's only now and

144

again you get them doing them all the same way like Jack the Ripper or Brides-in-the-Bath Smith. Two murders in six weeks in one little place! It would be a bit too much of a coincidence if it wasn't one man doing it. Both old ladies with money, too. Both church-mad. What else can it be?"

"Never in this world," said Mugger from his corner. "Old Griggs was murdered right enough. Couldn't be anything else when they put her in the grave and that. But this one's done for herself. You can make your minds up to that. Well, what else could she do? She was Past It, wasn't she? You can't blame her with a face like that."

"How can you talk like that, Fred Mugger?" said Mrs Chester. "Wicked I call it, with the poor lady not hardly cold yet. And I don't see where you all get your murders from. Bloodthirsty lot you seem to me. You can't even be sure old Griggs was murdered, really. Something might easily have fell on her. Look at that gargoyle that came down out of the church tower last year. It might have been something like that got her on the head. As for the other one, there's no reason at all to think it was murder."

"I don't see that, Mrs Chester," said Laddie Grey. "If Miss Griggs was killed accidentally how did she come to be buried in Chilling's grave where Rumble found her?"

"She was murdered all right," pronounced Rumble. "And very nearly so that no one was any the wiser. If I hadn't happened to notice how that grave wasn't so deep as I'd left it she'd be there now. She was murdered, but what I want to know is why? It wasn't just to take her bit of jewellery and money, that's certain. Then who had an interest in murdering her? And this one, too. We don't know what happens to Miss Vaillant's money. If we knew that we might know something."

"Oh talk sense, Rumble," said his wife. "What's the good of talking about Miss Vaillant being murdered when no one's been in there only poor Miss Flora Griggs and me? I've told you and I've told the police, the whole place was barred and bolted except the back door and I'd got the only key of that except hers. You're not going to tell me Flora Griggs did away with Miss Vaillant."

"I've always said those sleeping-pills are dangerous things," said George Larkin, unexpectedly joining the discussion. "You take a couple more than what the doctor tells you and you've had it. That's what she must have done because they say there was a whole empty packet in her bag."

For only the second time in his visits to the Black Horse, Carolus now heard the landlord's son speak.

"I think she was tight," said Bill Larkin.

"Whatever makes you say that?" asked Flo.

"She looked lately as though she'd been getting tight. You can always tell."

"You mean like me when I was going out with that fellow from Burley. Shall I ever forget it?" asked Flo. "Gin and pep, gin and pep, till I thought my breath would catch fire. But I didn't mind."

16

PENDING the report of the inquest on Grazia Vaillant, Carolus had no reason to go over to Gladhurst. The Spring Term was now well advanced and Carolus became absorbed in the exacting work of preparing boys for the Higher Certificate. He deliberately put aside his un-academic problems.

The news of the second death at Gladhurst had been prominently published in newspapers and it seemed that Mr Gorringer, the headmaster, was attempting, without actually addressing Carolus on the subject, to indicate reproach. There were curious head-shakings and clumsy shrugs while Mr Gorringer's "Ah, Deene . . ." when they met lacked all its customary gusto. Carolus supposed that the headmaster meant to suggest his displeasure with his Senior History Master who, having neglected the incidentals if not the essentials of school life in order to devote himself to investigation, had not been able to prevent the second death.

When Carolus either ignored these strange histrionics or appeared to put them down to some physical disorder and enquired after Mr Gorringer's health, the headmaster could keep silence no longer.

"Ah, Deene, Deene," he said, lugubriously. "I was deeply distressed to read of a second death at Gladhurst. Surely that might have been prevented? One could almost allow oneself the fell notion that death follows your investigations. I should be loath indeed to think such a thing."

"We don't even know what caused her death."

"Oh, quite. One must not be premature in supposing the worst. But I could have wished that in a case you were investigating the death roll could have been limited to one."

The headmaster passed on, his gown billowing, and Carolus made his way to his classroom.

Next day he received the *Burley Watchman* with a full account of the inquest on Grazia Vaillant. The Coroner, it appeared, had known his job and left nothing unprobed which could assist in revealing the full truth. Grazia had died of an overdose of the barbiturate which was used in Minerval tablets. An empty tube of these was found in her bag, bearing her finger-prints and hers only.

The pathologist who had conducted the post-mortem had also discovered a quantity of alcohol, probably swallowed in the form of gin and lime juice within a short time before death. The assumption was—though the Coroner stressed that it was no more than an assumption

147

—that Miss Vaillant had drunk a quantity of gin and lime sufficient to upset her judgment and had then swallowed the Minerval tablets.

Dr Pinton, the village doctor, gave evidence and said that he had been prescribing Minerval for Miss Vaillant for two years. She was a perfectly reliable patient who knew that she should never take more than one, or at the most two, tablets at a time. Asked if these tablets were particularly dangerous in conjunction with alcohol, the doctor said that this was so if either of the two was taken in excess. He had mentioned to Miss Vaillant that Minerval should not be taken after or with alcohol in any quantity, as he did whenever he prescribed Minerval, but he had done so more as a formality than anything else. He had never had any reason to suppose that Miss Vaillant drank more than a very occasional glass of wine with a meal. He was most surprised to hear the pathologist's report.

He described Grazia Vaillant as a woman whose feelings could sometimes be violent but who was usually well-disposed, perhaps rather gushingly so, in conversation. She was in no way abnormal, an enthusiast in religious matters but not a fanatic. He would not describe her as unbalanced. A little eccentric, perhaps, and exceptionally anxious to get her own way but not psychopathically so. He had prescribed Minerval for her because she lived so much on her nerves and energy that a tranquillizer at night was beneficial.

Asked how many tablets of Minerval he thought would be fatal he said that with the alcohol she had drunk he thought six would be sufficient, though death would not necessarily be immediate but would be preceded by first a period akin to inebriation, then coma, then death.

Mrs Rumble, eyeing the Coroner and everyone else with the greatest hostility, had given details of Miss Vaillant's private life. Asked if she had reason to think Miss Vaillant drank spirits when alone she said: " I don't know about spirits. She liked a drop of gin." However, she gave no details of the quantity purchased or where it was bought, only saying that she had seen gin in one of the cupboards and that though the empty bottles were always thrown away and the glass washed up, it didn't deceive her.

"Besides," she added, "Anybody doesn't get through all that lime juice in the middle of winter unless it's to drink with Something, do they?"

She recalled the two visits of Millicent Griggs just before that lady's death and said that 'as far as she could tell' the conversation had been amicable. She had noticed when she showed out Miss Griggs that she looked 'flushed up' and as though she'd 'had one or two' but she might have been mistaken. As for the visit from Miss Flora Griggs on the day of Miss Vaillant's death Mrs Rumble 'couldn't say much'. It was a Saturday and she was in a hurry to get off and do her week-end shopping. She had shown in Miss Flora and 'seen them settled without any words' in her presence. Asked if she meant the ladies hadn't spoken she looked at the Coroner as though she was sorry for his stupidity. 'Of course they spoke," she said. "I mean they had no Words while I was there." It dawned on the Coroner that this indicated not conversation in dumb-show but absence of any altercation, so the point was left behind.

Asked whether Miss Flora Griggs was still in the house when she left, Mrs Rumble said, yes. She had gone to the sitting-room where they were to say good-afternoon before leaving. She had already been paid. She found the two ladies looking a little 'worked up' if they knew what she meant, but she still heard no actual Words. Just as she came into the room she heard Miss Flora say something like 'your idols may be broken' and she had thought that sounded a bit nasty till she had heard it followed by Ezekiel something or other and realized that Miss Flora was only saying bits of the Old Testament as she often did. She wondered now whether it had referred to the new statue which Miss Vaillant had got down from London

149

and which was upstairs all in the sacking it had come in. Miss Vaillant had told her this was for the new Lady Chapel they were making in the church and the vicar had just agreed to it. Further she said that Miss Vaillant had seemed in good spirits lately and that she, Mrs Rumble, would never believe whatever anyone might say, that she had done away with herself on purpose. In her view, a drop of gin sometimes when you felt a bit low was one thing and taking your own life was another, a dictum which met no contradiction though the Coroner recalled the witness to the facts of the case rather than her own opinions.

The greatest surprises during the inquest were provided by a Mr Sturdis, a London solicitor who had handled the dead woman's affairs. Her real name, it appeared, was Grace Vallance and she was the daughter of a city outfitter who had wisely sold his business and premises before the great monopoly chain stores had pushed out small enterprise, He had retired to Folkestone with a comfortable fortune. He had accommodatingly died before dying had been made too expensive and Miss Vaillant had enjoyed an income, with all taxes paid, of some two thousand pounds a year to which she had added a thousand by progressive but slow reduction of capital. It was on his advice that she had adopted this course since she had no near relatives. The system had been calculated to provide a sufficient income however long Miss Vaillant's life might be and whatever further burdens of taxation might be laid on her shoulders. Mr Sturdis looked rather complacent about it.

Her will was a somewhat complicated one but the chief beneficiaries would be the Reverend Bonar Waddell and the Parish of St Jude, Gladhurst. There were conditions laid down for this, however, which might cause some difficulties, as for instance the introduction of incense during the service known as Sung Eucharist, the use of a Sanctus bell, something called Reservation for the Sick and a number of other changes which must be made in the church ritual before the local charities or the vicar himself could benefit under the will. A codicil had recently been added for the benefit of those charities, chiefly, Mr Sturdis understood, among the youth of the parish, sponsored by the Reverend Peter Slipper. These again were restricted by conditions. The Scout Troop, for instance, was to receive an annuity of £100 for the purchase of equipment, etc, but this was payable only if it could be shown that eighty per cent of the boys over fifteen were regular communicants. There was also a sum of £500 for Mrs Rumble.

It would be a difficult will to execute, Mr Sturdis said, and he did not envy the executors appointed, Commander Fyfe and Mr John Waygooze.

No evidence was given of any other caller at the Old Vicarage, either on the Saturday or during the evening or night.

The police said their piece, the vicar was called, then Miss Flora Griggs described her call on Grazia Vaillant at the latter's urgent request. Her evidence was somewhat confused and rhetorical, and really added very little to that already known. Miss Vaillant, she said, had *plied* her with strong drink, and when asked to be a little more explicit she let fly a covey of quotations from the Old Testament which seemed to confuse if not to embarrass the Coroner.

"Do you mean she poured out a drink for you?" he asked, trying to make poor Flora more specific.

"'Take the wine of the cup of this fury at my hand '," said Flora and the Coroner was puzzled till she added, "Jeremiah XXV, 15."

"Please be definite about this, Miss Griggs. Were you actually handed a glass containing gin?"

"I have no idea what it contained," said Flora. "I knew it was an abomination and would not take it in my hand."

"So two glasses had been poured out?"

"I think so."

151

"You refused them?"

"Most indignantly."

"Did you shortly leave the house?"

"I paused only to leave on the table some short tracts, which if this unfortunate woman would have turned in her wickedness and read, would have saved her soul alive."

"I see. And when you left she was in good health and spirits?"

"'Woe unto them that rise up early in the morning to follow strong drink; that tarry late into the night, till wine inflame them!' Isaiah V, 11."

"Do you mean that Miss Vaillant already showed the influence of alcohol?"

"She was a wine-bibber. That was sufficient."

The Coroner gave it up.

The verdict was eventually and inevitably one of Accidental Death by poisoning caused by an overdose of barbiturate.

For some days after this Carolus did not go over to Gladhurst and was interested to realize that five weeks had now passed from the date of Millicent Griggs's death. It was at least comforting to know that the police were taking as long as he was to reach any sort of conclusion. Now and again a daily newspaper would remind the public of this by talking about the unsolved mystery and recalling the fact, no doubt considered picturesque, that the body had been buried in an already dug grave. This had gripped Press imagination from the first.

One evening as he finished dinner in his home, Carolus had a surprise. Mrs Stick came in showing every sign of her most ardent disapproval.

"There's someone to see you," she said. "I've shown him into the little sitting-room because I didn't know what else to do, but I thought you said we weren't going to have any murderers and that coming here this time?"

"What's his name?"

"Griggs, he says, and it didn't take me long to know where I'd heard that name. I haven't said you're in yet, only that I'll go and see, so what shall I tell him?"

"Show him in, please, Mrs Stick."

"There! I knew it. And Stick and me just settling down to the television. Now we shall have to miss half the programme because I wouldn't turn the lights down with anyone like that in the house, not for anything."

"You could lock your door."

"It wouldn't be the Same Thing," said Mrs Stick and went out to usher in Dundas Griggs.

"Had a job to find you, old man," this one began.

"*You* had a job to find *me*?"

"Yes. I knew you taught here but I couldn't find out where you lived. In the end someone showed me the headmaster's house and I asked him."

"Oh."

"Inquisitive old character, isn't he? Wanted to know my name and business and everything. I nearly said I was a copper come to arrest you."

"I hope you did nothing of the sort," said Carolus, picturing Mr Gorringer as he received the news.

"No. I just said it was in connection with the Gladhurst Case."

"That was bad enough."

"Oh, I don't know. He seemed quite intrigued. 'Any new developments?' he asked in a stage whisper. I was just as corny. I put my finger on my lips. He nodded, and gave me your address. So here I am."

"Have a drink?"

"I don't mind. Dropper Scotch if you've got one. I've come to see you about something rather serious."

"Yes?"

"It's my Aunt Flora. She's in a bad state, old man."

"She seems to have been somewhat distressed at the inquest."

"It's since then. I don't know if she's going off her

153

rocker. She has started accusing herself now. Fortunately only in the household. But you never know where that will stop."

"Accusing herself of what?"

"What do you think? Murdering Grazia Vaillant, of course."

"But . . ."

"It appears that when she called on her that afternoon old Vaillant tried to get her to take a tot. Vaillant said, and for all I know it may have been true, that Millicent hadn't been above it on those last two occasions she called on her. Whether or not there was anything in this, she had backed the wrong horse with Flora. The old girl 'started like a guilty thing surprised' and almost threw it back in Vaillant's face."

"Yes. We know all this."

"But what you don't know is when Flora was a bit calmer she told Vaillant the best way of resisting the temptation to drink the awful stuff. Cheerio, by the way. If the terrible habit had such a grip on her that she couldn't resist, she was to take one of these dear little pills which Dr Pinton had prescribed and she would find herself asleep in ten minutes with all temptation gone. And she gave her a couple of Minerval tablets."

"But Grazia Vaillant was already taking Minerval."

"So it appears. But she never told Flora. Perhaps she didn't want to hurt her feelings. I don't know. Now Flora thinks she killed her."

"If those are her only grounds for thinking so, it's ridiculous."

"That's what I tell her. But she won't listen to me. Threatens to go to the police and give herself up."

"I shouldn't worry about that. Champer's cocky and self-important but he's not a half-wit. In murder cases the police often get quite a number of peculiar people accusing themselves. So long as all she has to confess is handing over two Minerval tablets, I don't think your aunt will be in trouble."

"You won't go and see her, then?"

"I don't think it's necessary. I'm pretty busy at the school just now. I warned Mrs Bobbin in the first place that this could only be a part-time job for me."

"There is another aspect of it, old man."

"Yes?"

"Flora's inclined to be a suicidal type."

"I hadn't heard that."

"Runs in the family. My grandfather, who built the Griggs Institute and what-not at Gladhurst, cut his own throat. They could get away with calling it an accident in those days. I shouldn't be a bit surprised to see Flora do something of the sort particularly if the police take no notice of her confession."

"Still, I don't quite see what I can do about it. You had better call in a psychiatrist."

"Think so? You may be right. Must do something. I thought at least I'd put it to you."

Carolus was wondering what it was he disliked about Dundas Griggs. His live-wiriness? Or his habit of saying 'old man'? No. Something deeper than those.

"I mean," added Griggs rather fatuously, "we don't want *another* death in Gladhurst, do we?"

"Personally, I didn't want any," said Carolus shortly.

"No. Of course. I meant. . . ."

"I think I understand what you meant. Have another drink?"

"Thanks. You see it's a bit uncomfortable when you stand to benefit."

"I suppose so."

"Not that there's likely to be much. If I know anything about Flora it will mostly go to her pet charities. But there's bound to be something."

"You feel that makes you a suspect?" said Carolus rather brutally.

"How can I be a suspect? The old girl's not even dead yet."

"Two women are."

155

"Yes. But . . . That's absurd, of course. No one could possibly. . . ."

"Most murders are like that, Mr Griggs. No one could *possibly* have done them. Yet always somebody has."

Dundas Griggs stood up.

"Thanks for the drink," he said. "I've said what I felt I ought to say. Since my aunt, Mrs Bobbin, consulted you, I mean. I'll run along."

Carolus showed him to the front door.

17

WHEN Carolus next went over to Gladhurst he found the Reverend Bonar Waddell in some perplexity.

"The testamentary dispositions of these two good ladies," said the vicar, "well-meaning and generous though they are, have given us all food for thought. Lawyers, executors, churchwardens and clergy, we are all concerned to follow their wishes as far as we are able and at the same time not to lose the little benefits for our parish institutions which they offer. My own share I would gladly sacrifice if it helped to provide a solution, but unhappily the same conditions apply to the church and parish charities as to the bequests to me."

"It must be very difficult for you," said Carolus, fascinated as usual by the vicar's agility in proceeding in two opposite directions at the same time.

"At a first glance," said Mr Waddell, "the conditions they lay down might seem to conflict one with another. Miss Griggs, for instance, stipulates that there shall be no Popish practices in the church while Miss Vaillant insists on the introduction of certain items . . . details . . . small etceteras of ritual. One has to realize at once the force of the word Popish. Far be it from me ever to introduce anything to which that word could justly apply. If I, for instance, were to appear in the *triregenum*, the tiara or triple crown worn by the Pope, with a cross ornamented on my shoe for the kisses of my congregation, I think there would be no doubt that I should be indulging in what Miss Griggs calls ' Popish practices ', but I cannot see that fulfilling the simple conditions laid down by Miss Vaillant can be held to be so."

" I see your point."

" Then Miss Griggs stipulates that there shall be ' no chanting of Masses '. Have I not frequently expostulated with Miss Vaillant against her use of that word with its most unfortunate associations? No, there shall certainly be no chanting of Masses. We have Sung Eucharist and that is quite enough.

" There is another seeming conflict. Both wills make reference to confession, Miss Vaillant insisting that the ' Sacrament of Confession ' shall be encouraged while Miss Griggs makes it a condition of her bounty that ' no confession boxes ' shall be seen in the church. We shall therefore have to do without any of those—in any case rather ugly—wooden erections which some Anglican and all Roman Catholic churches have installed. Then Miss Griggs, fortunately using somewhat archaic language, demands that there shall be no ' graven images ' in the church. She could be assured, if she were alive, good soul, that the life-sized statue which Miss Vaillant has purchased for our new Lady Chapel is certainly neither ' graven ' nor an ' image '; it is a plaster figure of Our Lady of Lourdes, admittedly purchased from the firm of Burns, Oates and Washburne, but Lourdes now has surely ceased to be a merely sectarian place of pilgrimage.

" None of the other little demands of Miss Vaillant conflicts with the conditions of Miss Griggs, the use of a Sanctus bell, the ringing of the Angelus, Reservation of the Sacrament, until we come to one which both ladies mention specifically and which puts us all in a quandary."

" What is that? " asked Carolus with genuine interest.

157

"Incense! " cried the vicar. "Miss Griggs says there must be none of that 'nauseous and Roman Catholic incense' in the church and Miss Vaillant makes the ceremonial use of incense at Sung Eucharist, at the Gospel, Offertory and Elevation, a condition for all her benevolence. What am I to do?" asked Mr Waddell.

"You should be able to see a way, surely," encouraged Carolus.

"I hope, perhaps I may have done so," said the vicar. "It is, you will observe, 'nauseous and Roman Catholic incense' which Miss Griggs objects to. We will have none of it. We will purchase our incense from the excellent old Anglican firm of Mowbray's which will be quite another matter. No one can then say that we are ignoring the wishes of either of the dead and the parish will benefit accordingly."

"Excellent," said Carolus in congratulation. "There was something else I wanted to ask you about. Laddie Grey and Naomi Chester are both, I believe, parishioners of yours?"

The vicar pursed his lips.

"They both live in the parish. Grey and his wife were married over at Breadley where she lived but I christened their child. Naomi Chester I do not often see in church."

"They hope one day to get married," said Carolus.

"That depends on a number of things," pronounced the vicar. "By the law of the land, Grey's wife's insanity does not provide grounds for divorce until the unfortunate woman has been confined as incurable for five years. That leaves nearly two years in which some change may take place."

"Then?"

"Then, if Grey is given a divorce, I shall have to decide whether or not I should be doing my duty in marrying him and Naomi Chester. On the one hand under the law of 1937 I cannot be compelled either to marry them or to allow their marriage to take place in my church. Convocations, indeed, have resolved that marriages of divorced persons should not take place in church. On the other hand civil law allows me to use my own discretion. I shall have to decide."

"Have you explained this to either of the parties?"

"I have had no occasion to do so."

"So that if they decide to take the matter into their own hands and simply start living together. . . ."

"Dear me! You alarm me, Deene. In my parish? I trust nothing of the sort would occur to them. It would set a most unfortunate example in a small community such as this. Really, I scarcely think you can be serious. Co-habit? Oh, no. I cannot suppose . . . The parents would surely dissuade them."

"Thank you, Mr Waddell. I just wanted to know the position."

His next call was at a pleasant-looking house at the lower end of the village. Here he asked for Dr Pinton.

"Was it private?" asked a smart young woman in nurse's uniform.

"Yes."

"Will you wait in here a minute? Dr Pinton's just finishing his National Health. He's had rather a rush this morning. Colds and sore throats."

The doctor was an active little man with pale rani-daean features and smooth thinning hair.

"Morning," he said, "What's the trouble?"

His big mouth worked like a trap.

"I'm sorry to take your time, Doctor. I'm that most irritating of all things—a private detective. Mrs Bobbin has asked me to try to find out about her sister's death."

"Oh, I see," croaked the doctor. Really he *did* look as though he had just come out of a pool. "Don't see how I can help. I had nothing to do with it."

"It was about these tranquillizing pills you prescribed for Grazia Vaillant."

"Best thing possible. Safe. Not habit-forming. Always prescribe them for neurotic old women. Nothing wrong with any of them except their nerves. Can't stand the pace

159

of modern life. Brought up to different standards. Find themselves harassed to death. Money worries. No servants. World upside down. What can you do? Give 'em tranquillizers."

"But isn't it rather dangerous, as in the case of Grazia Vaillant?"

"How was I to know she was on the booze? Of course it's dangerous if you take too many when you're tight. But normally, no. Have to understand these old middle-class women, Deene. They're damned annoyed with things as they are. They suddenly realize that the world has no use for them. Wants to see the back of them, in fact. They bumped them off in Russia and I'm not sure it wasn't more humane. We're just letting the species die out. Some of them can see that and are furious about it but there's no remedy. The least I can do is smooth their last years."

Carolus nodded.

"Old women! You never stop to think of them, do you? I don't mean only those from middle-class families but working class as well. Thirty, forty years ago the better-off ones had companions and went down to death selfishly, perhaps, but decently and without humiliations. The poor ones, even old widows of farm-workers, kept their own cottages to the last, when a cottage cost half-a-crown a week. Yes, and tottered round their little bits of garden and had visits from their grandchildren and perhaps their great-grandchildren, and made jam and home-made wine if they lived in the country and crept round to the pub with a jug sometimes if they lived in town. Now what happens? Herded into homes to sleep in dormitories and obey the rules like children. Or, if they've got enough money to keep them out of that, have the pestered, anxious, artificial existences that these old women here had. Do you blame old Mrs Bobbin, who has character, for being angry? Do you blame her sister for getting a sort of religious mania? Do you blame Grazia Vaillant for taking to the bottle, as apparently the old girl did, lately? Above all, do you blame me for pres-

160

cribing anything I can that gives them a few hours' worry-free sleep?"

"No," said Carolus. "I don't. But I would like to know for whom you prescribed it?"

"Only those who could afford it, unfortunately. The National Health Scheme won't run to Minerval. Millicent and Flora Griggs. Mrs Bobbin didn't need it. Grazia Vaillant. Agatha Waddell, sometimes. And of course Fyfe's wife."

"Why 'of course'?"

"Hypochondriac. Leads him the hell of a life."

"But he doesn't need Minerval himself?"

"Oh, yes. Fyfe takes tranquillizers. What do you expect? We're living in the atomic age, Mr Deene."

Carolus made no comment.

"Do you keep any check on these tubes of Minerval?"

"Only in the sense that I make a new prescription for each one and never give more than one in ten days."

"Never?"

"Well, as Gilbert says, well 'hardly ever'. There was an occasion, about a week before Millicent Griggs died, when she had lost her supply. Silly old thing had dropped it, or something. I gave her a second lot. But that was extremely rare."

"Tell me, as a matter of interest, do your confrères generally follow your practice in this?"

"Never discuss it. I should imagine so. This is much like any other village in Great Britain, Deene. You schoolmasters are still living in the pre-war age."

"Perhaps. Thank you for all you've told me."

But none of it, thought Carolus, did much to explain the one, the basic, the central fact of murder.

The telephone rang and Dr Pinton excused himself as he answered it, then rose to his feet.

"An accident," he said, "up at the church."

Carolus followed him from the house and got into his car, then decided to keep behind the Doctor on his way and see what had summoned him.

At the lych-gate was Rumble, for once without his grin. Dr Pinton pulled up short, jumped out and faced him.

"Where?"

"This way, Doctor."

Carolus followed them. The West door of the church stood open but in the early spring afternoon the interior looked gloomy. There seemed to be no one else present and Rumble made for a little door at the West end under the tower. This opened with a creak and revealed a spiral stone staircase.

Rumble switched on a light and started ascending, Pinton behind him and Carolus a slow last. It seemed a long ascent—spiral staircases always exaggerate the distance—but at last Carolus reached the place in which the bell cords were looped against the walls. The other two had already ascended farther and, pausing only a minute to notice the eight great swollen ropes, Carolus followed.

The staircase this time brought him to the bells themselves and he saw the two men leaning over someone on the ground. Beside them was Mrs Rumble, gaunt and serious.

Carolus could see that it was the figure of a woman on the ground and after a moment came near enough to recognize Flora Griggs. She was apparently unconscious.

Pinton saw Carolus.

"Will you please go and phone for an ambulance? 2244. Give my name and say it's urgent."

Carolus just had time to see a staircase, scarcely more than a ladder, ascending beside where the woman lay. This, he calculated, would lead to the open top of the tower.

"You can phone from the Old Vicarage," said Mrs Rumble, who had continued to 'keep the place decent' as she said. "I left the back door open."

Carolus hurried down and did as he had been asked. He entered through the silent kitchen of what had been

Grazia Vaillant's home and found the telephone in the hall. He gave his message.

He did not climb again to the belfry but waited to direct the ambulance men when they arrived. In a surprisingly short space of time the ambulance drew up and Carolus explained to two cool and efficient individuals in uniform that there had been an accident in the tower and that it was apparently a stretcher case.

Meanwhile the vicar had arrived, also Mrs Bobbin. He told them what he could and they all stood waiting for the stretcher to be brought down.

Just then Mr Slipper accompanied by two large Scouts came running up.

"I hear there's been an accident," he said. "I've brought Stanley and Cyril because they've both passed their First Aid tests."

The vicar raised his hand.

"Not now, Slipper. This is not the time."

"But . . ."

"No. No. Some less grave occasion, thank you. Send the boys home, there's a good fellow."

At that moment the two ambulance men appeared, bearing Flora Griggs on the stretcher. In a moment she was put in the ambulance and this disappeared swiftly in the direction of Burley.

"She'll be all right," said Dr Pinton. "But how on earth did it happen?"

Everyone seemed to turn towards Rumble and the vicar said, "I think perhaps we might discuss this in the vestry. This biting wind. . . ."

So Mrs Bobbin, the vicar, Rumble and his wife, Dr Pinton and Carolus went into the church. The vicar unlocked the vestry door and soon the little group was seated.

Rumble began at once.

"I don't know what made me follow her," he said. "She had a funny look, I thought."

"Funny?" queried the vicar.

163

"She looked as though she didn't hardly know what she was doing. I was in the garden at the time and I saw her come out of the front door, not seeming to know which way to take. So I got my jacket on, let her get a bit of a start and followed her."

"You should have called me," said Mrs Bobbin.

"I didn't know you were in. Anyway, off she went in the direction of the church. It gave me a turn to remember that it's not a few weeks since the other Miss Griggs must have come this way at about the same time and we all know what happened. . . ."

"Never mind that now," said the vicar sternly.

"Well, she came on, but not as though she was decided what she was doing as you might say. She seemed to stop here and look there till really I wondered whatever it meant. Then when she got to the gate of the church I didn't know what to think till she turned off suddenly to the left towards where her sister's buried in the new part and I understood what she was up to, or thought I did. She just wanted to visit her sister's grave."

"Get on, man, get on," said the vicar.

But this was Rumble's story and never in his life had he had such an attentive audience. He was not going to be hurried.

"She stood there for a minute, not interfering with anything, then she turned round before I knew where I was and marched off to the church door. I had to hop behind the old yew tree quick or she'd have seen me. But the funny thing was, I knew she was up to something when she went into the church. Don't ask me how I knew. Something told me."

Rumble paused dramatically and the vicar drummed on the vestry table. Then Rumble resumed.

"By the time I'd got to the church it was empty. Not a soul in sight. That really *did* make me feel queer. I looked everywhere for her. There wasn't a sign of her. I looked in the pews and behind the organ. I couldn't think for a minute wherever she could have gone. Then it dawned

164

on me. She'd gone up in the tower. But it shows how artful they are, doesn't it? She'd closed the door behind her. So I started up those stone steps as quick as I could."

"Could you hear anything?" asked Carolus.

"Not at first I couldn't. I got up as far as where the bell-ringers are and stopped for breath but there was still no sign of her. I went across to the door of the staircase that leads up to the bells and then I did think I heard something up ahead of me. So I shouted out 'Miss Griggs!' at the top of my voice. Whatever it was I heard seemed to stop. It was as quiet as a mouse up there and I hurried on to get to where the bells are and just as I was going round that blasted staircase I heard like a scream and a thud up above me. By the time I got to the belfry there she was on the floor just as you saw her."

"So what did you do?" asked the vicar.

"Do? It was a job to know what to do. She was breathing all right so I knew she was alive. I did the best I could. Put her as comfortable as possible and ran down all the way and across to the Old Vicarage to find my wife. Women are best for that job. She knew in a minute what was best to be done. 'Phone Dr Pinton', she said, 'and tell him what's happened. I'll go and look after her'. Then she grabs hold of a couple of cushions and takes a jug of water and she's gone. So I phoned Dr Pinton."

"You mean to say, then," said the vicar importantly, with a side-glance at Carolus, "that if someone was concealed in the tower and made an attempt on her life, he had an opportunity of getting clean away?"

"Oh, come," said Dr Pinton. "As far as I could see all Miss Griggs was suffering from was a little shock and a twisted ankle. Surely we needn't start imagining yet more murderers, need we, vicar?"

"I am the last to see things in a morbid light. But it did occur to me. What do you think, Mr Deene?"

Carolus said he agreed with the doctor.

"On the face of it it looks like an accident. The question of course remains of why Miss Griggs should wish to climb to the top of the tower at all."

"Ah, yes," said the vicar. "That indeed *is* a question. But doubtless all will be made clear in time."

Mrs Bobbin spoke sharply.

"I shall inform the police," she said and walked out of the vestry.

18

THE home which Carolus had purchased at Newminster when first he had taken up his post at the Queen's School was a small, charming Queen Anne house set amid other buildings but with a few yards between its walls and theirs. Behind it was a small walled garden, just now showing the earliest Spring bulbs.

Carolus loved his comfortable retreat, the first place he had found after the tragic death of his young wife. He knew that in their way the Sticks loved it, too, and for all their threats would not leave it or him. He decided, as he sat at lunch on a Saturday early in March and looked out on the signs of the soil's awakening, that he would make only one more journey to Gladhurst, then leave the village and the case to develop as it pleased.

He knew how the two women had died and it was now, as it had been from the first, a case somewhat repugnant to him. He did not want to be the means of hanging any-one over this, he wanted to disappear wholly from the scene and to forget it. But first, for his own satisfaction, he must clear up one or two small points at Gladhurst.

He hoped his lunch was finished and that Mrs Stick had gone to fetch the coffee but knowing her conviction that it was good for him to 'fill up with something sweet' he feared that his escape from the table would not be so easy.

"I've got a nice cream broolay for you," said Mrs Stick proudly. "I'll bring your coffee when I've seen you've had a good helping."

"I've decided to give up the Gladhurst case, Mrs Stick," said Carolus, as he helped himself gingerly to the *crème brulée* before him.

"That's good. You were only wasting your time and mixing with every Tom, Dick and Harry."

"I have to go over there once more, this afternoon, then I shan't go again."

"I don't know what you want to go at all for. I hear there's another one been pushed off the church tower now."

"You hear the most extraordinary stories. Miss Flora Griggs fell a few steps down the belfry ladder and twisted her ankle. She is already far better."

"Well, anyway, I suppose you know all about it, so why do you want to go over there again? "

"Not quite all."

"It's better than them coming here. You'll be back for your dinner, won't you? I've got a lovely bit of lamb for you—well, pray salay you could call it really."

"Keep it till tomorrow, Mrs Stick, I may be late tonight."

"Then you'll want sandwiches, I suppose? There's a little of the pattay left for them. You get back as soon as you can, Sir. I was only saying to Stick, we shall have you down again if you go on working like this."

Carolus, too, was glad that it was his last visit and that for the first time he was going to back out of a case before the results of his investigations were known. From the first, nausea and interest had gone together in his mind.

He was lucky enough, as he drove into Gladhurst at about half-past three that afternoon, to meet one of the people he most wanted to see.

"Naomi! " he called.

She turned, looked a little put out perhaps at the

167

familiar form of his address, then smiled in a friendly way.

"After me again? " she said. "I thought you weren't going to ask me any more questions."

"As a matter of fact I'm chucking the whole thing up. You won't see me here again. But come and have a cup of tea with me at Henson's. I've got something to tell you. And two things, both quite small, to ask you."

"All right," said Naomi.

Henson's the bakers, as Dundas Griggs had told Carolus, 'did teas' but it seemed to startle them somewhat when Carolus walked in with Naomi. They were shown to a room upstairs in which an oil-stove was quickly lit and gave out a strong smell and a weak heat. Carolus supposed that it was only the floor which was covered with linoleum —somehow there was an impression of it being every-where. But at least they were alone.

"Yes. I've decided to get out of it and leave the police to their own devices. And my strong belief is that those devices won't cause trouble to anyone."

"That's good," said Naomi, pouring out.

"I know the truth, pretty well," said Carolus, watching her steadily.

"I thought you did. Almost from the first."

"At the first it was only a guess. Now I think I've got it worked out."

"Oh, well," said Naomi dully.

"There's one thing I want to know and I think you can trust me. Did you actually *do* anything to her? "

There was no nonsense about Naomi. She did not pretend she wondered, as well she might have done, about which of the three ,women Carolus spoke. She looked back at him and her eyes were candid and perhaps a little scornful.

"I never touched her! " she said, then added quietly, almost mournfully, " it was only the bucket of water."

"Thank you. The other thing I want to know is—what did Millicent complain about? "

168

" The staircase," said Naomi.
" I see. Now it's all pretty clear."
" To you it may be. What about the police? "
" I am not in the confidence of Detective Inspector
Champer. In fact he greatly resents my interest in affairs
in Gladhurst. But from my observation of his procedure
and from what I know of the questions he has asked, I
do not think his theories in the various cases depart much
from what one must call the obvious. I think he is working on the supposition that Millicent Griggs was
murdered, as many another old lady has been of recent
years, for the sake of a few jewels and a sum of money,
the value of which had probably been exaggerated by
report. The fact that the jewels were left concealed does
not, I believe, preclude this theory for Inspector Champer
though it strongly suggests a local man. My guess at his
chief suspect would be Mugger unless he has found a
better among the inhabitants of Hellfire Corner. It is
difficult to see how he will get enough evidence to make
an arrest unless the numbers of some of Miss Griggs's
treasury notes are known. Even then, if they are traced to
any individual, there wouldn't seem to me much justifica-
tion for a charge of murder."
" Thank heavens for that."
" I think, Naomi, you've been a very silly girl. You
might have got others into trouble by behaving as you
have. But luckily, unless I am mistaken, the police will
write off Gladhurst as another unsolved crime and turn
to easier forms of prosecution."
" But you're doing almost the same."
" There is a difference in that I'm doing it having
satisfied myself that I know the truth. I want a last meeting with one or two of the people concerned, then I shall
disappear."
' One of the people concerned' was not Detective
Inspector Champer but he was the first person Carolus
met on leaving Henson's, Carolus knew it annoyed
Champer to be recognized as a policeman. He could not

surely think that his 'plain clothes' concealed his calling in this small village, but the habit of cultivating anonymity persisted. Carolus therefore greeted him cheerily.

"Good afternoon, Detective Inspector," he called. "How are you?"

He resisted the temptation to say 'how's tricks?' or 'booked any good reds lately?' or any of the more fatuous gags used in addressing policemen. The loud use of the man's rank was enough.

"Still here, then?" said Champer. "I thought you brilliant gentry saw through a little case like this in the first five minutes."

"As a matter of fact, I am pulling out, you will be glad to hear. Packing up. Finishing. One more evening at the Black Horse and I shall have left Gladhurst."

"Too hard a nut to crack, eh?"

"Oh, I have my little theory."

Champer gave a forced and throaty laugh.

"You have, eh? I bet it's something startling and original."

"Not really. It follows very much the conventional lines."

"You're not going to tell me you accept the police explanation of events? One murder, one attempted suicide, and one accident?"

"Yes," said Carolus. "As a matter of fact I do."

Champer laughed again.

"Well, I'm blowed," he said. "I never thought I'd meet a private detective who believed what was in front of his nose."

"I'd add that whoever may have been in the vicinity I have little doubt that Miss Flora Griggs was climbing the tower in order to throw herself off it."

"Better and better!" said Champer. "We don't seem to disagree on a point."

"I don't think we do," said Carolus; then, unable to resist a somewhat petty triumph he added: "In fact, there's only one difference. I know who was the murderer

170

and you don't. Good-bye, Inspector. We shan't meet again, on this case, anyway."

The last night Carolus intended to spend in the Black Horse would be, he hoped, a busy one. It was Saturday and there was no reason why he should not see most or all of those connected with the case. He arrived early and told George Larkin to let him know if either Commander Fyfe or Dundas Griggs went into the saloon bar.

George Larkin nodded but kept the taciturn silence he broke so rarely and sometimes so dramatically. This evening, after three minutes of staring thoughtfully at the counter, he showed which direction his thoughts had taken by remarking suddenly: " I've always said that stepladder in the tower was a danger."

" Oh, have you been up it? " asked Carolus.

George Larkin stared back and answered with the unwilling monosyllable, " Yes."

Rumble, who had entered in time to catch the gist of this, said, " So has that bloody police inspector. Looking at everything, he has been, as though he thought a murder had happened up there instead of a poor lady twisted her ankle."

" Oh? "

" Yes, and asking me questions about where I was and saying it happened at the same time of day as the other Miss Griggs, and I don't know what not. I'm sure he connects the two. Perhaps he thinks Miss Millicent Griggs was murdered in the tower."

" Like the little princes," said Carolus.

Flo entered and quickly became the centre of the conversation.

" I saw the ambulance," she began. " Couldn't help seeing it. . . ."

" Where? " interrupted Carolus.

" Trust you for asking awkward questions. I was just coming up Church Lane, if you *must* know. And it's no good you asking me who I was with because it's no business of yours. Though it wasn't Mugger, if that's what you think, but someone who's thought far more respectable. Not that I mind what he's thought. As I say I was coming up Church Lane and there was the ambulance and very soon out they come carrying poor old Flora Griggs on a stretcher. It was all I could do to stop laughing when I thought that last time she saw me she stopped me in the street and said, 'Upon every high hill and under every green tree, thou didst bow thyself playing the harlot', Jeremiah. That was a nice thing to say to anyone, wasn't it? Still I didn't wish her any harm, because I've always thought she was a bit touched, if the truth were known, and you can't take offence if someone doesn't know what they're saying, can you? "

" Did you know what had happened to her? "

" Not till later I didn't. Who'd have thought she'd have been larking about up in the tower at her time of life? Still, you never know what people get up to. I remember a fellow once wanted me to go into a church with him and *not* to get married. I said you wicked viper, fancy suggesting such a thing in a church. Shocking, I said, and so it was. Oh well, we must have a bit of a sing-song presently when Mrs Chester comes in. . . ."

Just then George Larkin informed Carolus that Commander Fyfe was in the Saloon Bar, and Carolus went round. He found the churchwarden looking very serious.

" Extraordinary thing, this about Flora Griggs," he confided.

" Where were you at the time, Commander Fyfe? I noticed you were on the scene within a few moments."

Fyfe looked with some hostility at Carolus.

" You noticed that, you say? I hope you noticed everything else that afternoon." He dropped his voice. " Rumble, for instance."

" What about Rumble? "

" One never knows, does one, in a place like this? What was he doing up in the tower? "

" You still haven't told me where you were."

"In the churchyard, as a matter of fact. Just seeing it was all in order. I heard the commotion and came up."

"I see."

"D'you know I'm almost sure I was followed here this evening? Very strange it was. Footsteps behind me all the way."

"Someone else could have been making for the Black Horse."

"Could have been. It's possible. It's one explanation. But ..."

He was interrupted by the entrance of Dundas Griggs.

"Just been to see the old lady in hospital. She'll be out tomorrow. Nothing but a sprained ankle."

Dundas Griggs acceded to a drink from Carolus and continued to discuss his aunt.

"Odd thing," he said, "but she seems enormously improved. The shock perhaps. Or the change of surroundings. She talked quite sensibly. Scarcely a reference to the Old Testament. She says she's looking forward to being back 'with Spring coming and everything'. She never seemed to notice anything as mundane as Spring before. It was a pleasure to see her."

"Did you discuss her accident?"

"Yes. She passed that off in a moment. 'It's all like a bad dream', she said, 'and I don't want to remember it. I can't even think now *why* I went to the church tower at all'."

"Splendid news," said Fyfe. "It still leaves a certain amount shrouded in mystery, doesn't it? I was telling Deene that I believe I was followed here this evening. You simply don't know in this place."

Back in the public bar Carolus found that Mugger had come in.

"I hear you're finishing with it," he said, his long pale face not changing its expression. "That's all very well for you but suppose the police get hold of someone innocent?"

"I don't think that's likely. Unless he was to try and pass a treasury note of which they had the number."

Mugger thought this over.

"You mean of the money the first one was supposed to be carrying?"

"Yes. The money carried by Miss Millicent Griggs."

"There was no money," said Mugger, not for the first time. "But if there had of been and anyone was to of found it, they wouldn't get themselves into trouble with spending a few old single pound notes not in series would they? So long as they burnt anything like a fiver there might have been?"

"I'm afraid I can't answer that. I've no experience."

"I shouldn't think they would," said Mugger. "Not if they wasn't in series. I mean, people have demands made on them. What can you do when they start theatening to go to anyone's old woman? I've never had anything like this one. The one I told you about. Works out at Ryley's Farm. It's give, give, give, all the time with this one. Mind you, I don't say she's not just right as they go, but you can't have them Asking the whole time, can you?"

"I'm sure your life must be full of difficulties."

"Well, it is just now. Then there's this other one. In Station Road. I don't know what to do about that."

The approach of Mrs Rumble drove Mugger off in a moment.

"I've got something to tell you," she whispered to Carolus. "I haven't told any of the others especially that Champer and as for Slatt I wouldn't think of it. It was when I was in the tower with Flora Griggs waiting for Rumble who'd gone to the telephone. She was unconscious when Rumble went away and again by the time he got back, but while he was away she Come To for a minute and I gave her a glass of water. Then what do you think she said? 'Now I *know* it wasn't me,' she said. That's all. But I thought you ought to know. Now, Rumble, don't you start trying to sing tonight and making a silly of yourself because you know you can't sing and that's all about it. You look as though you've had nearly enough, too."

Laddie Grey came across and silently handed Carolus a whisky, having observed what he was drinking.

"Naomi told me," he said comprehensively and with gratitude in his voice.

Mr Lovibond was also extremely polite.

"Sorry we shan't see you again," he said to Carolus. "It's a pity you couldn't find out who did it but I suppose you can't be successful every time," he added consolingly.

Then Mr Waddell came in for his Saturday-night visit and ordered the lemonade which he invariably drank here. His greetings were widespread and profuse and it took him some five minutes before he could reach Carolus, with whom he evidently wanted to speak.

"Good news, good news," he said. " I hear our respected and beloved Miss Flora Griggs is on the mend and in a far calmer state of mind than previously. I do not deny that her short absence has given us the opportunity we sought for installing our statue in the side chapel. I hope that when Miss Griggs sees the *fait accompli* she may become reconciled to it."

"Doubtful, is it? "

"I'm afraid so. Our Lady of Lourdes, you know. Our dear Miss Vaillant insisted on that and unfortunately purchased it from Burns, Oates and Washburne's. Had it been supplied by Mowbray's I should have felt on safer ground. But one small alteration I have thought it circumspect to make through the agency of our excellent stone-mason, Mr Baker. The statue as you know includes a rosary. This has been skilfully removed and the plaster repainted. I felt that though our dear Flora might be induced to accept the major premise, as it were, the rosary might have been too much for her."

"Very wise," said Carolus. " I'm not returning to Gladhurst after this evening. There is nothing more I can do here."

"Dear me. You leave us between two stools, as it were? "

"I think you will find that the most comfortable situation, vicar."

Carolus said good-night to each of his acquaintances and as he escaped from the bar he heard that Flo had had her way and a song began.

He found Slatt in high spirits.

"Hear you're beaten?" he said, grinning. "Found this one too much for you, did you? Oh, well, sometimes we're not as clever as we think we are."

"No," said Carolus. "Well, good-bye to you."

"Good-bye, Mr Deene. And if you should think who's done it you'll write to me, won't you?"

"Yes. I'll send you a p.c."

"What?" roared Slatt.

"A Police Officer. Er . . . a postcard. A telegram. Good-night."

"That's better," said Slatt, as Carolus drove away.

19

As Carolus predicted there was no arrest at Gladhurst and as the months passed the case was dropped by the Press and, save for a few people concerned, no one seemed to remember it. That Mrs Bobbin was very far from feeling reconciled was shown in the extremely angry letters she wrote Carolus from time to time. One would have thought from these that he was not only to blame for the unsolved mystery but for the murder itself.

Another who had not forgotten the affair was Mr Gorringer, the headmaster of the Queen's School, Newminster.

"Ah, Deene," he said, descending on Carolus in his gown and mortar-board, like some vast bird of prey fluttering down, "The end of term in sight at last. I

176

cannot deny that the vacation this year will be welcome."

"Yes," said Carolus, heading for the common-room.

But Mr Gorringer was not to be shaken off.

"You seem to have quite abandoned your investigation at Gladhurst. I cannot help asking myself why you should have done so without your customary *exposé* of the matter in the presence of those concerned."

"Wouldn't have been a good idea, this time. Perhaps too many *were* concerned."

"You mean you have discovered the truth, Deene, but you intend to keep it to yourself?"

"Yes, more or less."

"But can you reconcile that with your own conscience? A murder, after all, is a murder. I should have thought you felt called upon to inform the investigating police."

"Not really. The circumstances are somewhat unusual."

"I make no doubt of it. Is that not one more reason for revelation?"

"No." Carolus sadly saw the back of Hollingbourne passing through the archway which led to the common-room. "No," he said thoughtlessly to Mr Gorringer, "if you knew the whole thing. . . ."

"Ah, *if!*" cried the headmaster triumphantly. "But you haven't seen fit to confide in me, unfortunately."

"I've told no one," returned Carolus.

"I should hope not. It would surely be a grave discourtesy to reveal this matter to others before telling the facts to your headmaster."

"If you really want to know," said Carolus with exasperation, for his chair in the window and *The Times* had both been seized by now by Hollingbourne. "I'll tell you. Will you and your wife dine next Tuesday? I'll ask Lance and Phoebe Thomas."

"Unhappily Mrs Gorringer will have left Newminster by then. She is going to 'spy out the land', as she says, now that we have lost our customary holiday haven at Brighton. We may even go as far as Bournemouth, this year. My wife made one of her characteristically sprightly witticisms when I mentioned the place. 'So long as it's not an undiscovered country from whose Bournemouth no traveller returns,' she said. I laughed heartily. But your kind invitation, Deene, I may accept myself? Perhaps I might have the pleasure of meeting again that charming relative of yours. . . ."

"Fay? I'll see if she is free. About seven? Good."

Carolus almost ran across to the common-room. It was as he feared. Hollingbourne had inscribed 'Akbar' and 'dean' in different corners of the crossword. Both clues, Carolus felt instinctively, were wrong.

Tuesday came all too quickly. Fay arrived from town in the afternoon and Lance Thomas, the school doctor, a most popular and level-headed person, came with his wife Phoebe at a quarter to seven. At exactly five minutes to the hour Mr Gorringer made his entrance.

"Yes," he said, when greetings were over and he had taken a seat next to Fay Deene, " I will indulge myself in a dry martini. A most welcome suggestion."

Over drinks Carolus gave them the outline of the case as he knew it, not sparing them frank character sketches of Mugger and Flo for instance, but avoiding any word of elucidation. He wished them to be in possession of the facts, but his interpretation of these he kept for the hour after dinner. During the meal itself, he stipulated, they were to forget murder.

" An inspired suggestion of yours, my dear Deene," said Mr Gorringer enthusiastically. " Those of us who have, on previous happy occasions, experienced the Lucullan delights provided by your excellent Mrs Stick, will thank you for it. My ears still tingle when I think what she must have said once when I called her prawns in aspic a shrimp cocktail, a term only familiar to me from hearsay."

Carolus looked at those vast red organs so rich in bristles and wondered how they behaved when they tingled.

" Here is Mrs Stick," said Carolus. " No doubt she will tell you what she is going to give us."

"Well, I tried to make it a nice simple appetizing dinner, Sir," said Mrs Stick, addressing the headmaster. "Knowing you was to have a murder after it, as you might say. There's a consummay de vollile, some little lobster booshays because there was only the one lobster at Thompsons and I don't like going anywhere else. Then a bit of roast duck and a little sweet soofflay to finish with."

"Delectable," pronounced the headmaster. When Mrs Stick had left them he continued: "You are fortunate indeed, my dear Deene, in your employment of the Sticks. At School House, naturally, with thirty boarders, we have perforce a plainer regimen. Mrs Gorringer, in spite of the large staff we employ, tells me that even in the holidays it would be wellnigh impossible with all her culinary resources to provide her guests with a meal such as Mrs Stick creates single-handed. She can produce, she says in her inimitable way, quoting Dr Johnson, a good enough dinner but not a dinner to *ask* a man to. Your adroit housekeeper never fails you."

Nor was there anything to criticize in Mrs Stick's achievement that evening though she herself was not satisfied. "I thought the duck was done to death," she confided in Carolus afterwards and when he said "perhaps it was", she told him his mind ran on such things. She had meant it was over-cooked.

But at last came coffee and an old Armagnac, cigars, peace and expectation.

"Come, Deene. We are all ears. Who killed Millicent Griggs?"

"You will have found it strange that I retired from this case before revealing the truth. But to defend myself I must remind you of what kind of woman this was. Even her own sister, Mrs Bobbin, spoke of her as 'mean and sanctimonious' and said that she was 'unbearable' with Naomi Chester, 'inquisitive' with a 'mean and nasty mind'. The vicar's wife went further. Millicent was 'kind to no one but herself, generous only to gain her own ends', hypocritical, narrow-minded, self-centred and bigoted. She was also, Mrs Waddell said, capable of murder. Rumble, who was not an unkindly disposed man, used an unprintable word for her and added 'mean with her sisters and everyone else'. He was even more damning when he said—'always *right*, if you know what I mean. Do anyone a nasty turn'. Commander Fyfe said she was unpopular, 'a woman of insatiable curiosity of a most unsavoury kind'. The 'woman known as Flo', another critic wholly without malice, said Millicent had a 'nasty, dirty mind' and gave me examples of it which she said would 'turn me up' and I'm bound to say they nearly did. I had the impression from the first that Millicent Griggs was a horror and everything I heard about her confirmed it."

"Still," argued Mr Gorringer, "does that justify you in shielding her murderer, Deene? You have so often made it clear that murder itself, irrespective of the characters of perpetrator or victim, must be exposed. Where is the consistency in your behaviour?"

Carolus ignored this.

"Everyone spoke with frank dislike of Millicent," he went on, "except the one person of whom one would expect it, Naomi Chester. That roused my curiosity at once. Why did Naomi lie to me? What was she trying to conceal? Whom was she shielding? I started investigations with these questions very much in my mind.

"I had to do some spade-work which I have not bothered to record. That is one of the disadvantages of being at odds with the CID man investigating, as I was in this case. Had John Moore been in charge I should have been given details of the movements of certain persons which in this case I had to discover for myself.

"Though I never for a moment suspected Naomi of the murder of Millicent Griggs. . . ."

"Why not?" asked Dr Thomas.

"Well, Lance, one must allow something to one's instincts. Heaven knows I have had surprises enough in the cases I have investigated and am prepared to believe pretty well anything of anyone. I don't even say that I thought it impossible that Naomi should have bashed Millicent over the head—nothing in human nature seems impossible—but I do say that I could not suspect her of it. On the other hand she knew more than she would say.

"I was convinced moreover that it was through her that the body was disposed of, for it was fairly plain that Grey had been responsible for this. At about half-past three a telephone call was received for him at the home of Commander Fyfe, where he was working. The number of people who knew he was there must have been limited, for it had been arranged by Fyfe only on the previous evening. Mrs Fyfe thought the voice was that of an elderly woman—exactly the impression that would be given by a young woman trying to disguise her voice.

"Laddie Grey said that when he reached the phone no one answered, but it is noteworthy that he immediately packed up his work and left. Naomi was seen in the village by several witnesses who stressed that she was 'hurrying' towards her home. By her own admission Grey came to her home about four, or, it would seem, straight from his work.

"Whatever it was Naomi told Grey it was sufficient to set him in action. At half-past four a light was seen by Dundas Griggs in the house Crossways, but no one would answer his repeated ringing at the door. He walked round the house but found everything locked, even the garage.

"When Dundas Griggs returned to the house at 5.15 he found no light but heard what can only have been someone *who had a key of the back door* opening the garage from within and wheeling out a motor-cycle, locking the garage doors after him, wheeling a motor-cycle down the road and starting it up some yards away. I believe—and I will tell you why in a moment—that the person Griggs heard was Laddie Grey and that in the sidecar of his motor-bike was the body of Millicent Griggs.

181

"One must not count too much on witnesses' estimate of time but a few minutes later Mugger and the woman known as Flo were interrupted by a motor-cycle appearing at the top of Church Lane and throwing its single headlight on them. I know from Lovibond the electrician that Grey was short of a bulb in the light on his sidecar so there is no reason to think that the *single* light was not his. Seeing them he rode away and presumably returned later.

"It would rather naturally have occurred to Grey that the best place to get rid of a corpse was in the open grave in the churchyard for, as I heard from my useful informant Mr Lovibond, Grey used to help Rumble in his work as sexton. He would also have known where Rumble kept his spade and would have been in the furnace room a number of times.

"I was certain that Millicent was already dead when she was taken from Crossways, for a sheet had been snatched from one of the beds in order to staunch the blood. This sheet was found with her jewellery and money in the loft of the furnace room.

"Why, you may ask, if Grey had not murdered Millicent did he bother to remove her jewellery? Knowing Rumble's precision in the matter of the depths of graves he may have thought there was a chance at least of the body being discovered before Chilling's funeral, and played for safety. Robbery would be thought the motive and later he could remove and destroy the jewellery.

"He finished his task at about six, at least if the motor-bike which the vicar heard start up in Church Lane at that time was his. We know that it was an exceptionally dark night so it had not been difficult to keep his movements, except on his motor-bike, unseen.

"I never thought it very likely that Millicent left the house that afternoon, for someone would have seen her. The only reason suggested for her doing so was the church brass and this we know from Mrs Rumble had not been cleaned. But if her dead body had been taken, it occurred

182

to me, the shoes would have remained clean till she was put in the grave. It was thinking about this which caused me to make that lucky shot about galoshes. As soon as Naomi was asked she thought she had made a blunder. Instead of saying calmly that they were upstairs so that if Millicent went out that afternoon it was without them, she foolishly denied that they were in the house, then put them to be found at the back of the church. You may remember how confused she was when, an hour after my questions, I met her coming away from the church in which she had probably just dumped the galoshes.

"That was foolish. If Millicent had worn them to the church that afternoon she would not have removed them while she was cleaning the brass. And they certainly would not have remained unperceived by Mrs Rumble for several days, including the Saturday on which she cleaned the church.

"But again *why*? Why had Naomi put herself and the man she loved in this very serious danger if neither of them was guilty of the murder?

"Let us go back to that afternoon. Flora went out before half-past two, leaving Millicent and Naomi together in the house.

"Something caused Naomi to stay there after her time. Flora said the washing-up was done before she left. However conscientious Naomi might be I was sure that Millicent found some excuse to keep her there. Eventually, when she felt that I knew most of the truth, Naomi told me what it was. She complained about the staircase. Knowing her proclivity for asking questions, we may guess that she stood near the girl on the stairs, making one of her rather nasty cross-examinations. That was the tall stone staircase that rose from the hall. Then—'Did you actually *do* anything to her?' I asked Naomi. 'I never touched her', she said. '*It was only the bucket of water*'.

"In itself, you see, it was only what Millicent deserved, a bucket of dirty water thrown over her. But it had the most terrible consequences. The old woman, standing

183

probably a step or two lower than Naomi and receiving that water in her face, lost her balance, failed to find the balustrade with her hand as she fell, and tumbled backwards down the tall staircase to her death. Naomi, exasperated beyond patience, had meant only to throw water at her and as a result of it she found herself alone in the house with the dead body of Millicent. What she did then we know. Let's have a drink, shall we?"

It was nearly eleven o'clock and the five people in Carolus's sitting-room had scarcely moved for an hour. It was time to ease the tension and have a whisky or a brandy and soda.

20

MR Gorringer was of course the first to speak.

"In a sense I am relieved," he said, "that what appeared to be a terrible and violent crime was done without the baleful intentions one had feared. But . . ."

"But you feel it's rather an anti-climax, headmaster? What you had supposed murder was no more than an accident. Is that it?"

"Far be it from me to regret such a thing," said Mr Gorringer. "But I must say I had imagined something worse. Even when you had convinced me that Millicent Griggs died in her own house I imagined some intruder. . . ."

"In that case you will be yet more disappointed in the gruesome incident in the church tower."

"Gruesome indeed," postulated Mr Gorringer.

"Not so very gruesome," said Carolus, "except as it relates to the state of mind of Flora Griggs. And since it appears that she has quite recovered, that in itself concerns us less. In her last letter to me, in fact, Mrs Bobbin,

184

while showing that her resentment has in no way abated, speaks of Flora's happier and more level-headed state of mind as one of the few brighter aspects of the business. She is, Mrs Bobbin says, a completely different person and has developed something very like a sense of humour with which to view the bi-partisan antics of the vicar. This may be due to the shock of her fall, but I prefer to think that it has come about because she has been relieved of the baleful influence of the older sister. For many years she was under the malign domination of Millicent and now she begins to show her own pleasant character.

" Her fall, was of course, an accident but I'm afraid her intention in climbing the tower may have been suicidal. Whether or not she would in fact have carried out that intention it is not for us to judge. She passes out of the case, that rare and I must say welcome person, one who is better and happier for having been in contact with murder."

"So having disposed of these two most sinister-seeming mysteries as mere accidents," said Mr Gorringer loftily, "I suppose you will tell us that Grazia Vaillant committed suicide? "

"Oh no," said Carolus. "Grazia Vaillant was murdered."

The headmaster made a sound like ' Ttsschk! '

"That should have been obvious almost at once. Mrs Rumble told me that there was less than a third of a bottle of gin left in Grazia's cupboard. I doubt if Grazia, who by then was a fairly hardened gin-drinker, could have got drunk on that, or if drunk would have swallowed an over-dose of sleeping-pills. Besides, Minerval was more a habit of hers than gin, though she rarely took it in excess of one tablet at a time. Her last tube had been prescribed and bought from the chemist by Mrs Rumble a week before her death and contained ten tablets which, as Mrs Rumble said, 'she must have been taking' during that week. Mrs Rumble had noticed on the day previous to her death that there were only two tablets left in the tube. So that we can reasonably assume that all that could have been self-administered by Grazia Vaillant that evening was a third of a bottle of gin and two Minerval tablets. Or possibly three or even four Minerval tablets if she took the two which Flora Griggs gave her. These would probably have done her no harm and certainly would not have killed her.

" Besides, there is no reason to suspect her of wanting to take her own life. With the death of Millicent Griggs the long struggle for supremacy in the parish was ending in her favour. ' There was nothing wrong when I left that afternoon. In fact she was quite excited about getting a statue on the altar of the side-chapel'. So said Mrs Rumble and I see no reason, in this matter, to doubt her. No, Grazia was murdered.

" We know of only two people who were in her house that afternoon, Mrs Rumble and Miss Flora Griggs, but we have no means of knowing who, if anyone else, was admitted. On the other hand we can see how easy it was to poison her. She always had the same kind of gin and took the same kind of tranquillizers. A combined overdose of these two would be fatal. All a would-be murderer had to do was to provide himself or herself with a bottle containing the amount of Horsely's gin which approximately was left in Grazia's bottle and dissolve in it say half a dozen Minerval tablets. Grazia Vaillant mixed enough lime juice with her gin to kill the taste and would swallow this fatal mixture quite readily. It would not kill her at once but within an hour or two, unless she called assistance, she would be dead.

" She was anxious that no one should know she had taken to drinking gin in secret. That is the worst of this repulsive puritan doctrine of guilt about alcohol. Convince someone that it's wrong to drink, ignoring the lessons of the First Miracle and the Last Supper, and you can create a secretive drunkard, morally undermined, from someone who in openly enjoying a glass of wine would be a balanced and temperate person. Grazia's

186

secret guzzling of raw spirit disguised by *ersatz* lime juice laid her open to murder.

"What is more, the murder would be difficult to detect and almost impossible to prove. She herself could be relied on to throw the poisoned bottle into the deep well outside her back door where it would sink and lie with all the other bottles which had once contained Horsely's gin, the specially-shaped oval bottles so easy to slip into a bag or shopping basket. She herself would wash the glass which had contained the fatal mixture, as she always washed away the traces of gin before leaving the glass in the sink. And even if she were overcome before she had done these things, her murderer would be difficult indeed to identify.

"We knew, in this case, that the motive could not be simple robbery, as was suspected in the case of Millicent Griggs, for the house had not been broken into and nothing had been stolen. Although the expression on her face was one of fury it might merely have been at the thought of death. We know she grew violent when she had been drinking. And we had become accustomed to meeting very angry old ladies in this case.

"So for me it became, as these things so often are, a matter of motive. But a more complicated one than I had previously met. There were not the usual persons with obvious motives standing round, the relatives who would inherit money, the man remorselessly blackmailed, the third party in a love-triangle. The motives which one had to suggest for the murder of Grazia Vaillant were far-fetched.

"The only persons, so far as we know from the details given to the Coroner, who could be said to have expectations under Grazia's will were Mrs Rumble and the two clergy of the parish, the Reverend Bonar Waddell and the Reverend Peter Slipper. Unless you add persons who make suspicion fantastic, like those connected with the various church charities who would see them flourish, the choirmaster, the members of the Boy Scout Troup and so on, the two clergymen and the sexton's wife alone could benefit financially by Grazia's death.

"The only other possible motive seemed to be sheer hatred. We know that for years the sisters Griggs had hated Grazia Vaillant with all their natures and all the fervency of their religious beliefs, and that the surviving sister still hated her. We may suspect that Mrs Waddell nursed a strong detestation for Grazia. There may have been others whose hatred was better concealed. And since one at least of those who hated Grazia at the time of her death was a rich woman one could not altogether rule out the possibility of another person bribed.

"But in compensation for all this vagueness in the matter of motive I knew certainly the cause of Grazia's death and this gave me certain hard facts about the murderer. He or she had to have the following:

1. A knowledge that Grazia was secretly drinking Horsely's gin.
2. The knowledge that for some time she had been taking Minerval. (This, of course, so that when it was found she had died from an overdose, suicide would account for it.)
3. Access (even if only for a moment) to the cupboard in which she kept her gin.
4. Access to a sufficient quantity of Minerval.
5. The ingenuity to substitute poisoned for unpoisoned gin in an identical bottle.
6. An opportunity of doing so.
7. A motive.

"There was really only one person who fitted all seven conditions."

Carolus paused and lit a new cigar.

Mr Gorringer was the first to fall into his little trap.

"For once, Deene, you reduce speculation to a minimum. It was, of course, the unbalanced younger sister,

Miss Flora Griggs, who poisoned the unfortunate woman. You have mildly deceived us by suggesting that she has passed out of the affair."

"I don't think so," said Phoebe Thomas. "It was Mrs Rumble."

Carolus shook his head.

"Oh no," he said. "You might have ruled those out from the fact that I have dropped the case. It was Millicent Griggs."

"But . . ." began Mr Gorringer.

"I think you are forgetting," said Carolus firmly, "that very important information given me by Mrs Rumble which I scrupulously repeated to you before dinner. 'There was a bottle nearly a third full', she said on the morning Grazia was found dead. '*I told you she hadn't touched it since the other one died*'."

"Millicent Griggs went to see Grazia, not, I am convinced, for any wish for reconciliation but with about as much hatred and malice in her heart as a woman well could have. Millicent was, as we have already seen, a hateful and malicious woman. She came away from that first meeting and Mrs Rumble described her vividly—'All flushed up, she was, besides, I could smell her breath'. So after a lifetime's teetotalism, on which she held the strongest possible views, she had accepted some gin from Grazia. *Why?*

"Her words to her sister when she reached home were significant. Reported by Flora Griggs, they were 'she told me we should not for ever suffer, that we should be able to stand against the wiles of the devil'. Flora Griggs was sure that there had been no real reconciliation. Rumble, in fact, heard Millicent use stronger terms to Flora on that day when she returned from her last visit to Grazia. Woe unto the wicked, it shall be ill with her. For the doing of her hands shall be done unto her. But Millicent had seen the cupboard in which the gin was kept, had seen the characteristic Horsely's bottle. Moreover she knew from Dr Pinton that Minerval in conjunction with alcohol, both even mildly in excess, could prove fatal, for as Dr Pinton told the Coroner, he gave his warning whenever he prescribed Minerval, even when he regarded such a warning as no more than a formality. She had a way of revenge ready to her hand and to this bigoted and abnormal woman such a revenge was justified.

"That she put it into action we know. The manager of Forster's Stores in Burley said: 'the lady who was murdered'—he was referring to Millicent Griggs—'had been a customer of ours ever since I came to the shop as a boy. She has never been known to order anything alcoholic till about a week before her death. Then she came in and asked me for a bottle of the same'—that was Horsely's gin—'for purely medicinal purposes'. It would have been more accurate to say for purely homicidal purposes.

"During that week, too, she had to ask Dr Pinton for an extra supply of Minerval, giving the excuse of having lost her own. In reality she had used at least six, probably more tablets to doctor the gin which she was going to place in Grazia's cupboard during her second visit in place of the one she had seen there on her first.

"She had to depend on guesswork here and decide about how much gin there would be in the bottle by the time she paid her second visit. I think she judged well or was lucky, for Grazia never noticed it if the level was different.

"So she called again, armed with the large bag we have heard about, in which lay an oval bottle one-third full of Horsely's gin fortified with Minerval in lethal quantity. It was not difficult to change the bottles and depart. It was also an almost unprovable murder. If she had lived she could not, probably, have been charged with it, though she never dreamed that Grazia's death would be delayed by ten days and her own would intervene.

"But the fact that murder could never have been proved does not mean that it could not be fairly easily deduced. To anyone who had the facts of the case it

190

should not have been difficult to see not only that Grazia was murdered but by whom and how."

Mr Gorringer shook his head.

"I'm bound to say it eluded me," he admitted. "But in view of the evidence you have quoted, especially of the manager of Forster's Stores, I see that I was wrong in suspecting the younger sister. But in one little matter, Deene, you have surely deceived us. You described Detective Inspector Champer as saying to you derisively: 'You are not going to tell me you accept the police explanation of events? One murder, one attempted suicide and one accident?' To which you replied in the affirmative. Was not that almost . . . cheating?"

"Not at all. Those are exactly my explanations. But not in that order, headmaster."

"Bravo!" said Mr Gorringer and in a rare moment of abandon emptied his glass.